Sophie Loses the Lead

Other books in the growing Faithgirlz!™ library

The Faithgirlz!™ Bible
NIV Faithgirlz!™ Backpack Bible
My Faithgirlz!™ Journal

The Sophie Series

Sophie's World (Book One)
Sophie's Secret (Book Two)
Sophie and the Scoundrels (Book Three)
Sophie's Irish Showdown (Book Four)
Sophie's First Dance? (Book Five)
Sophie's Stormy Summer (Book Six)
Sophie Breaks the Code (Book Seven)
Sophie Tracks a Thief (Book Eight)
Sophie Flakes Out (Book Nine)
Sophie Loves Jimmy (Book Ten)
Sophie's Encore (Book Twelve)

Blog On Series

Grace Notes (Book One)
Love, Annie (Book Two)
Just Jazz (Book Three)
Storm Rising (Book Four)

Nonfiction

No Boys Allowed: Devotions for Girls
Girlz Rock: Devotions for You
Chick Chat: More Devotions for Girls
Shine On, Girl!: Devotions to Keep You Sparkling

Check out www.faithgirlz.com

faiThGirLz!™

Sophie Loses the Lead
Nancy Rue

zonder**kidz**

ZONDERVAN.COM/
AUTHOR**TRACKER**

The children's group of Zondervan

www.zonderkidz.com

Requests for information should be addressed to:
Zonderkidz, 5300 Patterson Ave. SE
Grand Rapids, Michigan 49530

Library of Congress Cataloging-in-Publication Data

Rue, Nancy N.
    Sophie loses the lead / Nancy Rue.
        p. cm. – (The Sophie series ; bk. 11) (Faithgirlz!)
    Summary: When Sophie suddenly shifts from being the leader of her student film project to playing a minor role, she resents not being in charge until she asks Jesus for help in accepting her new position.
        ISBN-13: 978-0-310-71026-4 (softcover)
        ISBN-10: 0-310-71026-X (softcover))
        [1. Video recordings–Production and direction–Fiction. 2. Conduct of life–Fiction. 3. Schools–Fiction. 4. Christian life–Fiction.] I. Title. II. Series: Rue, Nancy N. Sophie series ; bk. 11. III. Series: Faithgirlz!
PZ7.R88515Sjl 2006
[[Fic]–dc22
                                                                                              2006002195

Published in association with the literary agency of Alive Communications, Inc., 7680 Goddard Street, Suite 200, Colorado Springs, CO 80920.

Photography: Synergy Photographic/Brad Lampe
Illustrations: Grace Chen Design & Illustration
Art direction/design: Merit Alderink
Interior design: Susan Ambs
Interior composition: Ruth Bandstra

Printed in the United States of America

06 07 08 09 10 • 6 5 4 3 2 1

So we fix our eyes not on what is seen, but on what is unseen. For what is seen is temporary, but what is unseen is eternal.

— 2 Corinthians 4:18

That is gross," Sophie LaCroix said. She turned quickly and put her

hands over her friend Willoughby Wiley's eyes. If Willoughby saw the painting, she'd probably squeal like a poodle, the way she'd been doing all morning through the entire Chrysler Museum of Art.

"I think it's *cool*," Vincent said.

Sophie cocked her head at the painting, spilling her honey-colored hair against her cheek and squinting through her glasses. "No, it isn't," she said to Vincent.

"It's bloody and hideous."

"Is it totally disgusting?" Willoughby whispered.

"If you think somebody that just got their head cut off is disgusting, then, yeah," Vincent said. His voice cracked, just like it did on every other sentence he spoke.

Sophie dragged Willoughby toward the next room. Vincent shrugged his skinny shoulders and loped along beside them.

"Where's everybody else?" Willoughby said.

"They got ahead of us." Sophie looked up at Vincent as they passed through the doorway. "*They* didn't stop to look at some heinous picture of a headless person."

Fiona Bunting, Sophie's best friend, looked up from her notebook as Sophie and Willoughby headed toward her. "Oh — so you saw *John the Baptist*." She tucked back the wayward strand of golden-brown hair that was always falling over one gray eye and made a checkmark on the page. "That one's definitely repulsive."

"Does that mean it makes you want to throw up?" Willoughby narrowed her big eyes at Vincent. "You're not gonna say we should use *that* for our project, are you?"

Sophie shook her head. "No movies about people without heads. Who would play that part, anyway?"

Willoughby grabbed her throat.

"Actually," Vincent said, Adam's apple bobbing up and down, "there are some pretty cool ways we could make it *look* on film like somebody got his head cut off — "

"No!" all three girls said together. Sophie's voice squeaked, like it did when she was really making a point.

"Okay. Chill," Vincent said.

Sophie led the way to the next painting. She was the smallest of the Corn Flakes, as she and her five friends called themselves, but they mostly followed her. It had just been that way for the sixteen months since sixth grade when they'd gotten together and decided to be the group that was always themselves and never put anybody down.

"What's this one, Fiona?" Sophie said as they stopped at the next painting.

Above them was a portrait of a sober-faced lady in a gown that looked to Sophie like it weighed three hundred pounds.

"That dress is *fabulous!*" Willoughby said with a poodle-shriek. Her hazel eyes were again the size of Frisbees.

"Aw, man," Vincent said.

"What?" Jimmy Wythe came through a door from a room Sophie hadn't gone into yet. Nathan Coffey was behind him and plowed into Jimmy's back when he stopped in front of the painting. Jimmy looked at Sophie, his swimming-pool-blue eyes begging her. "It's gonna be kinda hard to do a movie about this painting."

"She's just sitting there," Nathan said. And then his face went the color of the inside of a watermelon. Sophie expected that. Nathan always got all red when he talked, which wasn't often.

"I'm gonna go find Kitty," Willoughby said. "She is going to *love* this."

"That's what I'm afraid of," Vincent said. "I guess we could pretend she's a corpse and make the movie a murder mystery."

Fiona rolled her eyes. "She is so not dead, Vincent."

Sophie looped her arm through Fiona's. "Let's go see if Kitty and them have found anything."

"Did they?" Sophie heard Vincent ask Jimmy as she and Fiona moved into the next room.

"It's all pretty much chick stuff," Jimmy said. "I mean, not that that's all bad."

"Not if you're a chick," Vincent said.

"They are so — *boys,*" Fiona said when they reached the room.

"Yeah, but at least they're not as bad as *some* boys."

That was why the Corn Flakes called Jimmy, Vincent, and Nathan the Lucky Charms — because they were way nicer than a couple of guys they referred to as the Fruit Loops. The Loops were famous for making disgusting noises with their armpits and trying to get away with launching spit missiles at people, stuff like that. Now that they'd been caught doing some really bad things, they didn't get by with as much, but they were still, to use Fiona's favorite word, heinous.

At the other end of the room, Willoughby was jabbering at light speed to the other three Corn Flakes.

"Is it a really pretty painting?" Kitty Munford said as Sophie and Fiona joined them. Her little china-doll face looked wistful. Kitty was back in school after being homeschooled while having chemotherapy for leukemia. It was as if everything were magic to Kitty in spite of her still-bald head and puffed-out cheeks.

"It's gorgeous," Willoughby said. "That dress was, like, to die for."

Darbie O'Grady hooked her reddish hair behind her ears and folded her lanky arms across her chest. "I bet the boys put the kibosh on that."

Sophie grinned. She loved it that even though Darbie had been in the United States for a year, she still used her Irish expressions. Between her fun way of saying things and Fiona's being a walking dictionary, the Corn Flakes practically had a language all their own. It was all about being their unique selves.

"Yeah, they hated it," Fiona said. "But we put the kibosh on John the Baptist with his head chopped off."

Kitty edged closer to Sophie until the brim on her tweed newsboy's cap brushed Sophie's cheek. "I don't want my first movie in forever to be about something gross."

"No way," Maggie LaQuita said. She shook her head until her Cuban-dark hair splashed into itself in the middle. "Kitty doesn't need that." In her stocky, no-nonsense way, she was protective of all the Corn Flakes, but especially Kitty.

"I like it that you're back with us," Sophie said to Kitty.

"This is like your first field trip in forever, huh?" Fiona said.

Willoughby raised her arms like she was going to burst into a cheer, but Maggie cut her off. Sophie was glad Maggie was the one who always enforced the rules. She would hate that job. She would have to keep her imagination totally under control to do that.

Right now, in fact, Sophie was searching for her next dream character. With a new film project to do for Art Appreciation class, she hoped one of the paintings would inspire her into a daydream that would lead to a new lead character that would shape a whole movie for Film Club to do. . . .

"Okay — now *that's* what *I'm* talkin' about!"

Sophie looked over at Vincent, who was three paintings inside the door, bobbing his head and pointing like he'd just discovered a new vaccine. Like a flock of hens, the Corn Flakes followed Sophie to see what he'd found. Darbie and Kitty stared, mouths gaping. Willoughby out-shrieked herself.

"We can't do a movie about this," Maggie said. Her words, as always, dropped out in thuds. "Those people are naked."

Nathan turned purple.

"Painters back then were all about the human body," Fiona said. "Don't get all appalled. It's just art."

"I don't even know what *appalled* means but I think I am that." Darbie shook her head at Vincent. "You're gone in the head if you think we're going to *touch* that idea."

Sophie suddenly felt squirmy. While the three boys wandered into the next exhibit room, Sophie put her arms out to gather her Corn Flakes around her. "You guys," she said, "we're acting like the Pops and Loops, all freaking out over naked people and talking about gross things being cool."

"*We're* not doing it," Maggie said. "The *boys* are."

"They can't help it," Sophie said. "They're just boys."

Willoughby gave a mini-shriek.

"I know what you're gonna say, Soph," Fiona said. "Even if they're being a little bit heinous, that doesn't mean we have to be."

"The Corn Pops *wish* they had Jimmy and those guys in their group," Willoughby said. She looked a little startled, curls springing out from under her headband. "Sorry — Corn Flake Code — I know we're not supposed to try to make people jealous and stuff."

Fiona sniffed. "We're so beyond that."

"Don't say anything else," Darbie said out of a small hole she formed at the corner of her mouth. "Here they come."

A group of four girls made such an entrance around the corner, Sophie was sure the paintings were going to start falling off the walls. Julia Cummings sailed in the lead with her thick dark auburn hair swinging from side to side and her glossy lips set in her usual I-smell-something-funny-and-I-think-it's-you curl. Fiona always said she looked disdainful.

She swept past the Corn Flakes with her three followers trailing after her, all dressed in variations of the skin-tight theme and curling their own lips as if they'd been studying Julia by the hour. There was a time when they would have stopped and made a remark about how lame and uncool each of the Corn Flakes was, but Sophie knew they didn't dare. The Corn Pops had been back in school for only a week since their last serious detention.

It was a sure thing they weren't going to take a chance with Mr. DiLoretto on their heels. He strode in right behind them, wearing his glasses with no rims and his curly grayish hair pulled back in a ponytail.

Sophie's high school sister, Lacie, had warned her about Mr. DiLoretto when the seventh graders switched from Life Skills to Art Appreciation for the new semester.

"He's a little weird," Lacie had said, "and he gets mad when people don't take art seriously."

So far, Sophie liked him fine because he let them choose their own groups for their assignment to do a creative project on any painting or sculpture they saw at this museum in Norfolk. And because he'd said their group could do a film. And because he was really nice to Kitty.

Even now he dodged the last of the Corn Pops and went straight to her.

"Have you done any sketches?" he asked. His voice was always edgy, it seemed to Sophie. Like he just knew that either excitement or disaster was around the next corner.

"I did a couple," Kitty said. She giggled and opened the red sketchbook she'd been carrying around. Sophie sidled closer and felt her brown eyes bulging.

Kitty's drawings looked just like some of the paintings they'd seen on the gallery tour. The lion in one looked like it was going to leap right off the page.

"Whoa," Maggie said. "I didn't know you could draw *that* good, Kitty."

"Kathryn is an exceptional young artist," Mr. DiLoretto said.

"Who's Kathryn?" Willoughby whispered to Sophie.

Kitty giggled again. Mr. DiLoretto swept the rest of them, including the nearby Corn Pops, with a bristly look. "Expect to see incredible work from her," he said.

With another proud gaze at Kitty, he hurried on, calling over his shoulder, "You have fifteen minutes left to choose your piece, and then we gather for lunch. Cuisine and Company is on your map."

"Hey," Vincent said from a doorway. "Get a load of *this* exhibit."

As the Corn Flakes headed for him, Sophie linked her arm through Kitty's. "You're gonna be a famous artist someday," she said. "There'll be, like, an entire museum of your paintings."

"I drew a lot when I was home, you know, 'cause there wasn't that much to do." Kitty hugged the sketchbook. "Now that I'm in remission, I can do a lot more."

"Mr. DiLoretto thinks you're, like, Leonardo da Vinci or somebody," Sophie said. She could hear her voice squeaking up into mouse-range. It did that when she was delighted too.

Another voice, not delighted at all, hissed from the direction of the naked-people painting, where the Corn Pops were standing in a knot.

"Pssst!" Anne-Stuart Riggins said.

Sophie was glad they weren't closer. Anne-Stuart had a continuous sinus problem, and sometimes her sounds came out wet.

"What do they want?" Kitty muttered.

"I remember when *I* was teacher's pet," Julia said.

"We *all* were," B.J. Schneider put in.

Julia gave her a green-eyed glare and went on. "It doesn't last, though. Teachers are fickle."

"Ignore them," Sophie whispered to Kitty. She nudged her by the elbow toward the door where the rest of the group had disappeared.

"I don't know, Julia," Anne-Stuart said. She gave a juicy sniff. "If Kitty kisses up to him enough, maybe he'll keep telling her she's ..."

She waved her hand at Cassie, who squinted her close-together eyes at the artist's name next to the nude painting and read, "Bo-ti–cel—"

"Whatever," Julia said.

"Yeah, whatever, Cassie," B.J. chimed in.

They *all* glared at B.J. this time, which gave Sophie a chance to give Kitty the final push through the doorway.

"They're always so jealous of each other," Kitty whispered. "I'm so glad I'm not a Pop anymore."

"I'm glad you're not too," Sophie said. "You never have to worry about us being all jealous and stuff."

"Sophie—look at this!"

Sophie hurried over to where the Film Club was standing, staring up at a painting of a can of Campbell's soup.

"Who would paint a stupid soup can?" Maggie said.

Fiona tapped her pen on her notebook. "Some guy named Andy Warhol."

"All his stuff is weird," Vincent said. "This one's, like, a stack of boxes."

Sophie gazed at it. "Look how real that looks."

"You thought that lady in the beautiful *dress* was boring," Willoughby said. "This would put you to sleep."

"Not movie material," Vincent said.

"If somebody was, like, *under* the boxes getting crushed," Nathan said, "that would be cool."

"That would be repulsive," Fiona said.

Sophie pulled a strand of her hair under her nose. She was glad it was long enough to do that again, because it always helped her think. Personally, she liked the funny paintings of boxes and soup cans.

"What do you think of Andy Warhol's work?"

Sophie looked up at Mr. DiLoretto.

"It's—I like it," Sophie said.

"Why?" he asked.

Lacie had been right, Sophie thought. He *was* a little bit weird. She adjusted her glasses and looked back at the soup can. "Well," she said, "it's all just ordinary stuff, but up there on the wall, all shiny and perfect, it seems like it's special too."

"Well, well."

Uh-oh, Sophie thought. Did she say the wrong thing? What was it Lacie had said about him getting mad when people didn't get art?

"You have the beginnings of a good critical mind," Mr. DiLoretto said.

Sophie let go of the hair she was still pulling under her nose like a mustache. "I do?" she said.

"You don't have an ounce of talent for drawing or painting, but you show some promise as an art critic." He glanced at his watch. "Nine minutes 'til lunch . . ."

Sophie didn't hear the rest of what he said. She was gazing again at the giant soup can — *and pawing through her large canvas artsy-looking bag for her notebook and pen. Ah, there they were, beneath the camera and the portable tape recorder and her calendar full of appointments with people who wanted her expert opinion on modern art.*

So many demands on my time, *Artista Picassa thought.* But I must make some notes on this piece because it fascinates me.

Very few people had her appreciation for the more bizarre artists like Andy Warhol. It was her duty to educate people, which was why she was an art critic. And possibly the most famous one in all of Virginia, if not beyond —

That was it, of course. Maggie could write it all down in the Treasure Book later.

They would do their project on one of Andy Warhol's pieces.

She could play Artista Picassa, the famous art critic. . . .

And maybe artists who were jealous because she didn't praise their paintings would do something heinous. . . .

Too bad they couldn't use Pops and Loops in their film. They'd be perfect as envious painters.

Sophie looked around for her group, but there was nobody left in the exhibit room.

"Rats!" Sophie said to the soup can.

She dashed into the hall, but she didn't have a clue which way to go, and the map of the museum was shoved into the bottom of her backpack.

Where's Maggie when you need her? she thought. *Maggie probably had the whole layout memorized by now.*

But that was why Maggie was the club's recorder and Sophie was the director. Creative people needed organized people to keep them from getting lost, Sophie decided.

The smell of food and the clattering of forks finally led her in the right direction. Mr. DiLoretto was standing in the doorway of Cuisine and Company, glaring at her from under his tangled eyebrows.

"I got caught up appreciating art," Sophie said.

He just pointed her inside. Fiona waved to her from a table across the room.

"Mr. DiLoretto wouldn't let us look for you," she said as Sophie slid into a chair.

"Tell her what we decided," Vincent said to Fiona.

"You're gonna love this, Soph," Jimmy said. His usually shy smile was wide.

Sophie looked at Fiona. "Decided about what?"

"The film," Fiona said. "Jimmy found the perfect painting for our project."

Something about the way Fiona didn't quite look back at Sophie made Sophie feel squirmy. Slipping off her shoes, Sophie pushed her toes between the close-together bars under the chair.

Maggie pushed a bowl of green soup toward her and said, "Eat."

"It looks re — what was that word?" Willoughby said.

"Repulsive," Darbie said. "It tastes better than it looks."

"It's called *The Surgeon*," Vincent said.

"The soup?" Sophie said.

"No, the painting."

"What painting?"

"The one we're going to do our project on," Fiona said.

Sophie twitched, pushing her toes farther between the tight bars, shoving them past the balls of her feet. The group had already decided? Without her?

"It's not boring at all," Willoughby said.

"And there's no blood and guts," Maggie said.

Kitty giggled. "Or naked people."

"But it's still way cool," Nathan said.

If he turned red, Sophie didn't notice. She was sure she herself was losing all color. She felt her body go rigid, and she pushed down hard again with her feet.

"I haven't even seen it," she said.

"After this, we get to go to the gift shop," Jimmy said, "and I'm gonna get a poster of it."

"All right, folks," Mr. DiLoretto said as he wove among the tables, "it's time to move on to the museum shop."

"Sophie hasn't even eaten yet," Maggie said.

"Well, now, that's her problem, isn't it?" Mr. DiLoretto said. "Kitty, you'll come with me. I want you to meet one of the artists who teaches classes here."

"Don't worry, Sophie," Darbie said, pronouncing it "Soophie" like she always did. "I've got some snacks in my bag you can eat on the bus."

Sophie didn't feel like eating. All she wanted to do was grab Fiona in the hall and find out just exactly what was going on.

But when she tried to get out of her chair, she couldn't. Her feet were stuck in the bars, and they weren't coming out.

Come on, Soph, " Fiona said. "Mr. DiLoretto's already mad because you were late for lunch—"

"I can't!" Sophie whispered. She tried again to pull her feet out, but they just stayed there and throbbed.

"What's going on?" Maggie said, voice thudding for all to hear.

Sophie clamped her teeth together. "My feet are stuck. Could you get me out so he doesn't see this?"

But before Darbie and Fiona could even hit the floor to inspect, Mr. DiLoretto was on the scene. One look at Sophie's feet, and his voice went straight to its edge. Sophie cringed. He had obviously seen the disaster he'd always known was coming.

"I bet if we put some butter on her foot we could slide it right out," Fiona said. She was already reaching for the pat on Sophie's bread plate.

"*We* aren't going to do anything," Mr. DiLoretto said. "*You* are going to the museum shop, and *I* am going to find a maintenance man."

"Yeah," Vincent said, nodding at Sophie's feet. "Somebody's going to have to cut those bars. I'd say you're going to have to use at least a—"

"Out!" Mr. DiLoretto shouted.

Yeah, Sophie decided. This had definitely taken him over the edge.

Everybody broke for the door, the Corn Flakes looking back at Sophie like she was about to have a leg amputated. The Corn Pops were much less sympathetic. B.J. snorted right out loud.

"I'm really sorry," Sophie said to Mr. DiLoretto.

"You're the one who's going to miss out on shopping," he said.

"But you wanted to take Kitty to meet that artist—"

The sharp cut of Mr. DiLoretto's eyes made her wish she hadn't reminded him. She chewed on the ends of her hair—until she saw a mountain-sized man in a denim shirt approaching carrying a toolbox. Sophie tossed her hair aside before she could chomp off a hunk and swallow it in fear.

The man scowled, and Mr. DiLoretto glared, and they exchanged remarks about kids not being able to just sit in chairs like normal people, as if Sophie weren't even there. Once she was sure the guy wasn't going to take her foot off at the ankle, all she could think about was what Daddy was going to say. She hadn't been in trouble for a really long time, but that didn't mean he wouldn't still take her video camera away, and all that neat film-editing stuff he'd bought her for Christmas, especially if—

"Will I have to pay for the chair?" Sophie said. Her voice sounded tiny even to her.

"Nah," the man said. "With all the kids we get coming through here, stuff like this happens."

"Not with *my* people," Mr. DiLoretto said.

Sophie was sure she wasn't one of *his* people. All she wanted to do was get to *her* people.

By the time the mountain man got the bars cut and Mr. DiLoretto did a two-second check to make sure Sophie's ankles weren't hurt, everybody was finished in the museum shop and had boarded the bus. Sophie made her way down the aisle amid posters being unrolled and kids passing bracelets and key chains to each other. The Flakes and Charms *would* have to sit all the way in the back. By the time she got to them, she felt like one of the weirder paintings in the gallery with everyone gaping at her.

"Sophie, are you *okay*?" Willoughby said when she finally made it to the last seat.

"Let me see your feet," Darbie said. She smacked her own thighs for Sophie to prop up her feet.

"How big was the saw they used?" Vincent said.

Sophie expected him to lick his chops any minute.

"This'll cheer you up." Jimmy was grinning so big it looked to Sophie like there was an extra set of his perfect teeth. Even his very-blond hair looked excited.

"He's jazzed," Fiona said to Sophie.

"Show her, Jim," Willoughby said.

Jimmy unrolled the poster like it was a royal banner, and Fiona helped him hold it in place.

"Isn't it the *best*?" she said.

It wasn't a Campbell's soup can, that was for sure.

There was a lot going on in the piece, including two men looking into another man's ear, another man having his arm bandaged by a very large woman, and a dog passing through. There were pots and pitchers and bowls all over the place, all bathed in light stream-ing through a window.

"You haven't heard the coolest part yet," Vincent said.

He nudged Maggie, who gave him a black look. Maggie would hardly let one of the Corn Flakes touch her, much less an actual boy.

But Sophie forgot that the minute Maggie opened the special Treasure Book the Flakes wrote important things in. The page she turned to already had her neat handwriting on it.

Sophie stared. "You started planning the film?"

"We're just getting ideas," Darbie said.

Kitty made a little circle on Sophie's jacket sleeve with her fin-gertip. "We wouldn't *decide* anything without you."

"Yeah, but these are great ideas." Vincent poked Maggie again. "Tell her."

This time Maggie scooted away from him, which was hard since they were sitting three to a seat on either side of the aisle. Fiona and Jimmy were on their knees on the second to last seat, facing backward so they could hold up the poster. Sophie wriggled uneasily, and not just because she was crammed between Kitty and Willoughby. It felt as if someone were sitting in *her* place. As the bus lurched, so did everything in Sophie's head. Nothing was the way it was supposed to be.

"Here's what we have so far," Maggie said. "'The painting is called *The Surgeon*, and it's by David Ten-ee-ears the Younger.'"

"He was a painter in the baroque period," Fiona said.

Willoughby yelped. "Whatever that is."

"Get to the good part," Vincent said.

He was starting to remind Sophie of the cafeteria monitor, the way he was snapping out orders.

"'In our movie,'" Maggie read from the Treasure Book, "'the painter will be played by Kitty since she's the most artistic.'"

"I don't mind playing a boy," Kitty said. She pointed to her head. "I have the hair for it."

"You don't have *any* hair," Nathan said. He turned crimson even before anybody could glare at him.

Maggie read on. "'The painter gets kidnapped by another painter who's jealous of her talent.'"

"That's Jimmy," Fiona said. She jabbed him with her elbow, and he jabbed her back.

It's like they have a secret together, Sophie thought. She gnawed at a hunk of her hair.

"'Nathan will play his evil assistant,'" Maggie read.

"He won't have that many lines," Vincent said. "That way he can do a lot of the editing since he's good at it."

"You didn't say that before." Maggie's dark eyebrows drew together. "Do you want me to write that down?"

"Not now," Fiona said. "Get to the really good part."

Jimmy grinned at her. "You mean *your* part."

Huh, Sophie thought. It sure *sounded* like they'd been deciding.

"'An expert comes in,'" Maggie read on.

Ah. Artista Picassa. Maybe this wouldn't be so bad—

"That's me," Fiona said.

"We picked her because she can say the big words without making a bags of it," Darbie said.

So can I! Sophie wanted to say. And Mr. DiLoretto had said *she* could actually be an art critic, for real.

But Sophie just chewed on her hair. They were sure to get to her part any second now, even if it wasn't Artista Picassa. She wasn't *that* attached to her yet.

Maggie went back to the Treasure Book. "'Fiona the art expert will find the clues to where Kitty the painter is—in the painting itself.'"

"This is where it really gets cool," Jimmy said.

Maggie ran her finger down the page. "'We'll set it in the ba-rock period.'"

"Ba-roke," Fiona said. "Like it rhymes with choke."

Willoughby bounced on the seat beside Sophie. "Maggie's gonna come up with fabulous costumes for her mom to make, and I get to do hair and makeup." She poodle-yipped in Jimmy's direction. "Jimmy even said he'd wear tights."

Nathan turned red.

"Vincent and I are going to do the filming," Darbie said.

Vincent nodded. "Now that we have two cameras—Sophie's and the school's—plus all our editing equipment."

"*Our* editing equipment?" Sophie said.

"Well, yours, plus the stuff Mr. Stires has." Vincent looked at Willoughby. "Go ahead and say it."

Willoughby shrieked. "It's going to be *fabulous*!"

Every face around Sophie was shining as if a painter had cast them all in some golden light. Sophie stopped squirming and let her hair drop from her mouth.

"O-kay," she said. "I can direct that. You guys did good."

Suddenly nobody was looking at her—except Vincent, who said, "Actually, I'm going to direct it."

"Since it was mostly his idea," Fiona said. She glanced at Sophie, and then studied the painting as if she'd never seen it before.

Sophie swallowed a lumpy thing in her throat. "Okay—well—since it was his idea." She straightened her tiny shoulders. "So, Fiona, when do we start writing?"

Fiona looked at Jimmy—who glanced at Darbie—who bulged her eyes at Maggie.

"*What?*" Sophie said.

"We kind of already started writing it while we were waiting for you," Fiona said.

"We?" Sophie said.

"Me and Jimmy."

"They couldn't just sit here," Darbie said. "You know how they are, Sophie."

Sophie *thought* she knew how they were. But right now, sitting in what felt like the wrong spot, watching her friends fill in all the spaces that belonged to her, she wasn't so sure.

She looked at Maggie. Wasn't there a rule about this that Maggie ought to be pointing out about now?

Maggie frowned at the page. Sophie watched her hopefully, until Maggie looked at Vincent and said, "What's Sophie's part?"

"We didn't get that far yet." Fiona's voice sounded too high. "But I'm thinking she should be my servant boy."

Maggie put her purple gel pen to the page and mouthed as she wrote S-E-R—

"What does your servant boy do?" Sophie knew her voice was squeaking into only-dogs-can-hear range, but she couldn't help it. Squeaking and disbelief went together.

Fiona cleared her throat. "Back then—"

"'In the ba-roke period,'" Maggie read from the book.

"The servant helped the mistress get dressed, brought her tea, turned down her bed—"

"Then why would your servant be a boy?" Darbie said.

For the first time since she'd gotten on the bus, Sophie was grateful to one of them. It wasn't that she hadn't played boy roles before. She could play anything. And Kitty was being a good sport about her part as the male painter. But if there was no reason to be a boy—

"I'll be a servant *girl*," Sophie said. "And my name will be Johanna Van Raggs."

Fiona tucked a wayward hair strand behind her ear. "We haven't started picking names yet."

"Except David Ten-Ears the Younger," Maggie said.

Kitty giggled.

"Not 'Ten-Ears,'" Fiona said.

"Oh, let's call him that," Darbie said. "It'll be a gas!"

"We're gonna have to get serious about this," Vincent said, "if we want this film to be — " He looked at Willoughby.

"Fabulous!" she said.

"I *am* serious," Sophie said. She aimed her gaze at Fiona. "I want my name to be Johanna Van Raggs."

"It's kind of fancy for a servant girl," Fiona said.

"It's not that big of a deal," Vincent said. "It's not like anybody's actually going to say her whole name in the movie anyway."

"I like it," Kitty said. She looped her arms around Sophie's and leaned her head on her shoulder. "I wish you were gonna be *my* servant."

"Hey, wait," Jimmy said. "She could be Kitty's — David's servant — and when David gets kidnapped, Fiona could make — what's her name? — Joanne? Fiona could make her help her."

"My character would so have her own servant," Fiona said.

"But she'd use David Ten-Ears' servant because Joanne would know more about him — where he might go, stuff like that," Jimmy said.

Vincent's eyes took on a gleam. "Besides, then you could really order her around, Fiona. Y'know, treat her like your slave. Put that down, Maggie."

"Hello!" Sophie said.

Fiona leaned across the aisle toward Sophie, shaking her head. "It's not like I'm gonna bop you over the head or something, Soph."

"That'd be cool, though!" Nathan said.

"No!" Kitty and Willoughby said in unison.

Before Sophie could even say anything over the stereo squeals in her ears, Vincent said, "No violence — but let's go with Jimmy's idea."

"That'll be a bigger part for you, Sophie," Darbie said. She looked to Sophie like she'd just burped some of that repulsive green soup, and it tasted worse this time.

"It's not about who has the biggest part anyway," Fiona said.

"Can I see that book you bought, Fiona?" Willoughby said quickly. "I want to look at the hairstyles."

It seemed to Sophie that all the girls — except Maggie — were talking in way-high voices. Like maybe if they sounded "up," Sophie wouldn't be so down.

But as Sophie stared out the bus window and watched the signs on I-64 herald their approach to the Poquoson turn-off, she sank low enough to crawl under the seat. What had just happened?

She always came up with the ideas for their films.

She always dreamed up the main character and played her in the movie.

She and Fiona — or sometimes *she* and Darbie, and once *she* and Jimmy — had always written the scripts.

And there had never been any question that *she* would direct.

After all, wasn't she the one who had gotten her own camera and started making films of her daydreams with just Fiona and then Maggie, and later Kitty and then Willoughby?

If it wasn't for her, would there even be a Film Club? Would the Lucky Charms even have people to make amazing videos with?

"You okay, Soph?" Willoughby said.

"Hey, Sophie," Jimmy said, "don't forget, we have Round Table at lunch tomorrow."

"I got you something at the gift shop," Fiona said. "I hate that you didn't get to go."

"Want some crackers, Soph?" Darbie said.

Sophie tried to smile, but she had a hard time making it happen. They loved her — she knew that — but why didn't they remember who she was?

There was only one thing to do, she decided as the bus pulled up in front of the school. That was to show her fellow Flakes and the Charms that they needed her to be in charge.

Because if she wasn't Sophie LaCroix, the great film director — who was she?

Sophie's six-year-old brother, Zeke, met her at the kitchen door when she

got home. His face was smeared with jelly, and so was the doorknob, the front of the refrigerator, and the whole snack bar.

"Are you finger-painting with jam?" Sophie said.

Zeke scowled at her. Sophie grabbed his hand just before he dragged it across his sticking-up-all-over-the-place dark hair. He looked just like their father, minus the strawberry preserves.

"No," he said. "I was makin' me a sandwich."

"Where's Lacie?" Sophie said. "It's her day to play with you."

"She's not home yet," he said. "But I'm old enough to make my own snack."

"Yeah," Sophie said, "but you're not old enough to paint the kitchen when you're done. Does Mama know you're doing this?"

"No." Zeke climbed onto a stool at the snack bar where two pieces of bread were drowning in jelly. "I'm makin' her one too. It's a surprise."

"That's for sure," Sophie said.

She was headed for the sponge when Zeke said, "Mama said she wants you to come up as soon as you get here." He narrowed his blue-like-Daddy's eyes suspiciously. "You're not gonna tell her about the surprise, are you?"

"No," Sophie said. Her mind was going in another direction as she climbed the stairs. Had Mr. DiLoretto already called Mama about the chair incident?

She paused before she opened the door to Mama and Daddy's bedroom. Mama was pregnant, and things weren't going so well. If they didn't want Baby Girl LaCroix to arrive before her time in March, six weeks from now, Mama had to stay in bed. Daddy had told the three kids a bajillion times that Mama wasn't supposed to get upset.

Maybe I should have told Mr. DiLoretto that, Sophie thought.

"Is that you, Soph?" Mama called.

She didn't sound like she was going to throw a lamp or anything. Not that Mama ever had, but Sophie had figured out that being pregnant definitely made a person cranky, even soft Mama.

Sophie opened the door a crack and peeked in. Mama's usually wispy face, which people said was just like Sophie's, was puffy and white like the inside of one of Mama's homemade biscuits. Not that she'd baked any in a while. Her brown-like-Sophie's eyes were saggy and tired-looking, even though it seemed to Sophie that she took a lot of naps. Her hair, curly and highlighted, was now mostly Sophie-brown with some gray and was pulled up into a messy bun on top of her head.

Still, she smiled and held out her hand. It used to remind Sophie of an elf's hand, but now the fingers were swollen like little sausages. "Come in, Dream Girl. I've been missing you."

Sophie felt like Jell-O inside as she crossed to Mama's bed. There wasn't a sign that she'd talked to Mr. DiLoretto. And she'd called her Dream Girl, which meant at least *somebody* remembered who Sophie was.

"How was the field trip?" Mama asked.

"Horrible!" Sophie said.

Before she could stop herself, she'd knelt down and laid her head beside Mama on the bed, and Mama was stroking her hair. Sophie poured out the awfulness of everything, from the evil chair to the way her Corn Flakes had let the Film Club give her nothing but the lamest role in life.

Mama made sounds, little "oh's" and small "ah's" and tiny "ouches." By the time Sophie was through, she was all the way up on the bed, snuggled next to the baby sister inside. Even she seemed to be listening.

"I don't know what to do," Sophie said.

"Want some help?" Mama said.

But before Sophie could even sit up, the door opened and Lacie burst in. She was holding a telltale jelly-stained towel, which she thrust behind her back. Sophie knew the everything's-fine smile she pasted on was fake.

"Sorry I'm late, Mama," Lacie said.

"Did Zeke tear the house apart?" Mama said.

"Of course not. But Soph, I do need some help with—dinner."

Sophie saw the set of Lacie's jaw, which made her look like Daddy too. That, and the way she was flipping her dark ponytail, was a clear signal for Sophie to get downstairs and help her sandblast the kitchen.

Sophie scrambled from the bed and headed for the door.

"Sophie," Mama said, "we'll talk some more later. Be sure to tell God about it, okay?"

Lacie led Sophie down the stairs, speaking low and tight. "Did you not see the mess he made down there?"

"Mama wanted to talk to me."

"Yeah, well, while you were having your little chat, Zeke dropped that whole jar, and it broke. There's jam all the way into the dining room."

"Aw, man!" Sophie said. "I'll help you clean it up."

"No — you keep Zeke away from me so I don't do him some kind of bodily harm. I'll clean it up before Daddy sees it."

Lacie wasn't kidding about the mess. There were even drippy strawberries on the kitchen ceiling. Sophie ducked out with Zeke in tow before one could drop on her. The day had been bad enough without having something gunky fall into her hair.

"I didn't get to take Mama the snack I made her," Zeke wailed as Sophie dragged him into the family room.

"Nobody can eat that much jelly, Z-Boy," Sophie said. "What video do you want to watch?"

Zeke picked a Spider-Man cartoon, and while he watched it for what Sophie was sure was the two-hundredth time, she tried to do what Mama said. She closed her eyes and looked for the kind eyes of Jesus.

It was a way of praying that she'd learned from Dr. Peter. He was the cooler-than-any-other-grown-up-on-the-planet therapist Sophie used to see every week, back when she didn't get her work done in school and daydreamed herself into trouble all the time. After she mostly got her act together, he became the Bible study teacher at church for the preteen girls.

Since Sophie was so good at imagining, Dr. Peter had taught her to get very quiet and imagine Jesus was right there with her, which, he told her, Jesus actually was, and just talk to him. Sophie didn't ever imagine Jesus answering her. Dr. Peter said that would be like writing a script for the Lord. But somehow, in ways that Sophie never would have thought up, he did answer, usually later, when Sophie least expected it.

As soon as she curled up into the corner of the sofa, eyes closed, Sophie could feel Jesus close to her. His kind eyes came right into view in her mind, soft and gentle, and understanding everything she told him.

About how unfair things were all of a sudden, and how she wasn't as important as she had been that morning when she woke up.

The thing is, she told him without words, *being the director is what you made me for. Right?*

Sophie sat with that for a moment. Of course that was right. Why else were all their films so cool? What other reason could there be for the way the Flakes got closer and closer every time they made one?

Sophie kept her eyes shut as she smiled. She'd just have to show the Flakes *and* the Charms that they'd made a mistake by taking her job away from her. The question was how to do that without breaking the Corn Flake Code about not hurting people's feelings.

She wished that for once Jesus' answer would just pop up on a billboard right away. Sophie scrunched deeper into the pillows and tried to shut out the Spider-Man theme song.

Her Corn Flakes were pretty smart, especially Fiona and Darbie. They would probably figure it out as soon as things started going wrong in rehearsals, wouldn't they?

She tried to see Jesus' kind eyes, but she was already pretty sure he was saying yes.

So she was in an almost normal-Sophie mood the next morning when she got to school. When Mrs. Clayton, one of her history/language arts teachers, reminded her first period that there was a Round Table meeting at lunchtime, she started to feel important again.

Round Table was the special council made up of two seventh graders — Sophie and Jimmy — and two eighth graders, and two teachers — Mrs. Clayton and Coach Nanini, a boys' PE teacher who looked like a big bald-headed bear and called Sophie "Little Bit." The council tried to help kids who couldn't seem to follow the rules, because there was almost always a reason why people acted out. Round Table was doing a lot to stop bullying at GMMS. Sophie and Jimmy had even set up a website about cyberbullying.

Sophie couldn't wait to get there that day, especially since all the Flakes and Charms could talk about during third-period PE was the new movie. Nobody showed signs of seeing that Sophie should be the director. Even in fourth-period math, Vincent passed her a note that said, "We need to edit at your house in two weeks. Put it on your calendar."

Sophie didn't write back. She couldn't think of a nice way to say, "Don't worry about it, Vincent. You won't be in charge that much longer."

When Sophie and Jimmy got to the Round Table conference room, Mrs. Clayton and Coach Nanini were in the corner talking to Mr. Benchley, the principal. Hannah and Oliver, the two eighth graders, were in their regular places. As Sophie slipped into her chair, Hannah leaned across Oliver, eyes batting at her contact lenses, and whispered, "Something's about to go down."

"What?" Jimmy said.

"I don't know, but check out Coach Nanini's face."

Sophie looked. Coach Nanini was a bigger man than even her father, who used to play football. That, along with his arm muscles being like two hams, was why Sophie thought of him as "Coach Virile." With his shaved head and heavy eyebrows, he could look like a television wrestler, but when he was helping some kid with a problem, which he did a lot, he was more like a cuddly stuffed animal.

But right now, his cheeks sagged, and his bright eyes drooped at the corners.

"He looks like we're at a funeral," Oliver said. "Who died?"

"Shut up!" Hannah said.

Sophie did as the three adults took their seats. She tried to catch Coach Nanini's eye so she could get him to grin at her, but he kept his gaze on his thick knuckles.

Yikes, maybe somebody *did* die.

Mr. Benchley folded his hands on the table and smiled that smile principals used when they were about to say something for a kid's own good.

What's he doing here anyway? Jimmy wrote on Sophie's notebook.

Sophie shrugged.

"I'm so proud of what you've done on this council," Mr. Benchley said. "Not only have you helped a number of students straighten out, but you've grown as young adults yourselves."

Sophie smiled, but she could hear a *however* in there somewhere.

"I'm eager to have more students experience the Round Table as you have," he went on. He stroked his salt-and-pepper-colored beard like he was petting a cat. "Which is why I've advised Mrs. Clayton and Coach Nanini to start with a new council each semester."

Sophie looked at Coach Virile, but he was still examining his fist. Mrs. Clayton's face had gone as stiff as her dyed blonde helmet of hair. Sophie was sure *advised* meant Mr. Benchley had given them an order.

"So that means we're out and four other kids are in?" Oliver said.

"It means you're going to get a much-deserved rest, and four other students will be given the same opportunities you've had."

"Starting when?" Hannah said.

Mr. Benchley smiled like there was actually something to smile about. "Starting now. Coach Nanini and Mrs. Clayton have already selected the new members."

Coach Nanini lifted his eyes and pressed his mouth into a sad line that made Sophie think of Charlie Brown.

"This is in no way a reflection of your work on the Round Table," Mrs. Clayton said. Her trumpet voice sounded more like a somber flute today. "You four have done an exceptional job."

"So — we're really off the council now?" Sophie said.

"Do you want them to write you a memo?" Oliver said.

Hannah poked him. "So who are our replacements?"

Sophie didn't want to hear the names. That would make it way too real.

But Mrs. Clayton read them anyway. Two eighth graders, and Ross Marley, who was a friend of the Charms, and Darbie O'Grady.

"Those are good people," Jimmy said.

"Yes," Sophie said. But she felt like a crumpled-up piece of paper.

One thing was clear as she worked her way through the hall crowd to her locker: it was more pressing than ever that the Film Club figure out she should be director. If one more important thing was taken away from her, she might just disappear completely.

The Flakes were all at their lockers when Sophie got there. Fiona's gray eyes went round when she saw her.

"Soph, what's wrong?" she said. "Did you have some kind of heinous case at Round Table?"

Sophie pulled her locker open and stuck her head inside. She didn't want Darbie to see her about-to-crumple face. When she did find out her good news, she'd realize it was Sophie's bad news. Sophie knew she'd probably offer to let her have her place.

That was the way Corn Flakes were — and it would be hard to say no.

"What's the deal, Soph?" Fiona said behind her.

"Just a minute," Sophie said. "I'm looking for something."

That was the truth. Right after winter break, all the Corn Flakes had decorated the insides of their lockers. Just about everybody in school was doing it, in fact. It made going there six times a day not so bad.

Sophie looked at the pictures she'd taped in hers and tried to find the old Sophie — the one who before yesterday felt pretty good about her life. She looked back at herself as characters like Goodsy, the cop in disguise; and Louisa Lockhart, Victorian lady.

When she got to the photo Coach Nanini had taken of her at a Round Table meeting, she pulled it off and stuck it in her pocket.

4

Sophie swallowed the lumpy thing in her throat and pulled her head out of her locker.

"You okay?" Fiona asked.

"I'll tell you later," Sophie said.

Fiona nodded. "We have a lot to tell you too. We got tons done at the Film Club meeting." She turned her head and said over her shoulder, "Come on, you guys, we have to fill Sophie in."

But Kitty, Maggie, and Willoughby were at the other end of the locker row with Darbie, who was reading something from a piece of paper.

"That rocks, Darbie!" Willoughby shrieked.

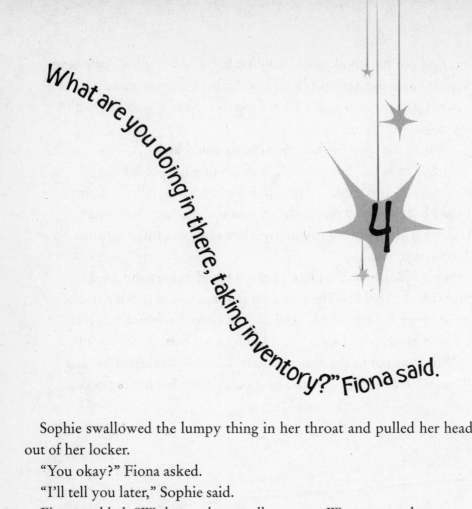

"Does Sophie still get to be on it?" Kitty said.

Fiona turned to Sophie with question marks in her eyes. Sophie just shook her head.

Then she put on a smile and joined in the mini-celebration with Darbie, although she couldn't quite bring herself to bounce up and down like Kitty and Willoughby. When Willoughby started making up a cheer to Darbie, Fiona pulled Sophie away.

Sophie wanted to hug her for that. She could tell Fiona how losing Round Table left a hole in her, and she'd understand and not tell Darbie.

But before she could even start, Fiona said, "I wanted to tell you the new stuff we decided about the movie, and now there's no time."

"Oh," Sophie said.

"Okay, here's the plan." Fiona hooked her arm through Sophie's and half dragged her toward Mr. Stires' science room. "I'll get a restroom pass, and you get one, and we'll talk for, like, five minutes in the bathroom. Mr. Stires won't care. We always get our work done."

Fiona didn't wait for Sophie to agree. She just gave Sophie's arm a squeeze and hurried to her seat. Sophie fell into hers just as the bell rang. Darbie flew through the door before it stopped.

"You're lucky, Darbie," Mr. Stires said. His voice, his toothbrush mustache, even the shiny dome that erupted from his fringe of hair — everything about him was cheerful, like always. "New rule here at GMMS."

In the back of the room, Tod Ravelli and Colton Messik, the two Fruit Loops, groaned like they'd just eaten a whole pig.

"It's not my rule," Mr. Stires said, "but since it was handed down by Mr. Benchley, I'm going to enforce it."

"So it's about being tardy," Darbie said, "since I almost was."

"Excellent reasoning," Mr. Stires said.

"So what's the rule?" Anne-Stuart said with the usual sniff.

"Three tardies in a class means an automatic detention."

Sophie let out a long breath. At least she didn't have to worry about that. She was never tardy.

But we're going to get more people coming up before Round Table, she thought.

And then she sagged miserably in her seat. She didn't have to worry about that either.

Mr. Stires gave the assignment, and the class settled down to pretending to read while they complained to each other about the new rule. Fiona nudged Sophie and went up to Mr. Stires' desk. Sophie heard her whisper to him, but he didn't write out a pass.

"One more thing, class," he said.

"Another rule?" Julia arched an eyebrow at him as if he wouldn't dare.

"Another rule. Mr. Benchley has also started a bathroom log."

"A what?" the class said in unison.

"Every time you receive a pass to the restroom, your teacher will enter it into the computer."

"That's against my civil rights!" Colton rose in his seat, ears sticking out comically from his head. "Isn't it?"

"No," Vincent told him.

"Once you have used six bathroom passes," Mr. Stires said, "you're done for the semester."

"Six in each class," Anne-Stuart said, nodding her silky blonde head like she expected Mr. Stires to nod with her.

"No, ma'am," Mr. Stires said. "Six for all your classes put together."

"What if we have to throw up?" somebody said.

"What if we have diarrhea?"

While the class named off every disease that required a toilet, Fiona held out her hand to Mr. Stires and said, "That's okay. I'll take my first one now."

She gave Sophie a you-*are*-coming-aren't-you? look as she went out the door.

But Sophie just opened her science book and shoved a hunk of hair into her mouth. Maybe it wasn't a good idea to use up a bathroom pass. Besides, she didn't want to hear any more news that was going to make the lump in her throat even bigger.

It was big enough for one day.

On Monday, Sophie was glad rehearsals for the film project would start in Mr. Stires' room during lunch. She'd spent a boring weekend doing nothing but homework and Zeke-watching. Every time she called Fiona, just so she wouldn't go mad (as Darbie would put it), she got Fiona's answering machine.

Mr. Stires and Miss Imes, the math teacher, were their Film Club advisers, but mostly they let the group work on their own. And Sophie figured out right away that Fiona and Jimmy had spent the whole weekend writing the script.

She could imagine them sitting by the fire in Fiona's living room with the Treasure Book, and Fiona's grandfather Boppa letting them toast marshmallows when they took breaks, and Fiona's doctor-mother ordering Chinese food for them, and Fiona having moo goo gai pan — Sophie and Fiona's best-friends favorite.

When she got to the part in her mind where Fiona and Jimmy were high-fiving each other over a great line they'd just thought of, she had to turn off her imagination. That wasn't easy to do. Especially when, halfway through Film Club's first read-through, Sophie realized something.

"Excuse me," she said.

Vincent blinked at her over the top of his copy. "It's not your line, Sophie."

"I know," Sophie said. "So far, I don't *have* any lines."

Kitty patted Sophie's arm. "We're not done. You'll have some."

"But I'm in *this* scene, and I'm not saying a word."

"That's because we decided to make the maid mute," Fiona said.

"Like a deaf mute?" Maggie said.

"No, she can hear. She just can't talk." She turned to Sophie. "It'll be a way more interesting character, Soph, with lots to do."

Willoughby gave a nervous yip. "At least you won't have any trouble learning your lines, Soph."

"I never have trouble learning my lines!"

"That's true," Maggie said. "She doesn't."

Fiona rolled her eyes. "That's not why we did it this way."

Sophie wished Darbie would ask why they *did* practically make her invisible in the movie, since Darbie was the only one standing up for her these days.

But Darbie was at her first Round Table meeting. Sophie didn't even want to go there in her mind. She flipped through the script again.

"So if I don't ever speak," she said, "how do I help find the clues in the painting for Fiona?"

"You mean Leona," Fiona said.

"Her character's name is Leona Artalini," Maggie said.

"I *know*." Sophie didn't comment that she thought it was the stupidest name she'd ever heard of.

"It's Italian," Jimmy said. "Some of the best artists came from Italy, so we figured — "

"Could somebody just answer my question?" Sophie said.

Vincent's big loose mouth twisted up. "What *was* your question?"

"How is Johanna Van Raggs supposed to help Leona whatever-her-name-is find the clues in the painting if she can't talk?"

Fiona propped her elbow on Sophie's shoulder and gave her a patient look. "Soph," she said, "Johanna's not the art expert; she's a servant. Leona figures out the clues. Johanna just waits on her while she's doing it." She looked at Jimmy. "Feel free to jump in any time."

A red blotch had appeared at the top of each of his cheeks. "It just seemed like it would be funny if you couldn't talk. There's a place where you use all these hand motions to try to tell her something, and she keeps thinking you're saying something else."

Fiona nodded her head until the stubborn strip of hair popped out from behind her ear. "It's really hilarious, Soph. It's in, like, scene five — "

"Which we're never gonna get to if we stop and talk about every single thing." Vincent looked up at the clock. "Fiona, it's your line."

Just about every line is Fiona's line, Sophie thought. She grabbed a hunk of hair and chowed down.

They were allowed to work on the project every day during sixth period, Mr. DiLoretto's class, which gave them more in-school time than they usually had for their Film Club movies. The only problem was that they had to stay inside the classroom — where everybody else was working with their groups too. Including the Loops-Pops bunch.

For their project, they appeared to be putting together some kind of poster about a painting called *Ship of Fools*, which, Darbie murmured to Sophie one day, was perfect for them. Since all they were doing was cutting out pictures from magazines and coloring in letters, they had plenty of time to observe the Flakes-Charms at work.

During the first rehearsal of the kidnapping scene, where all Sophie did was hide behind a chair, Anne-Stuart said to her, "Is Jimmy supposed to be a gangster or something?"

"Sort of," Sophie said.

Anne-Stuart gave a particularly juicy sniff. "He doesn't even look like a bad guy. He's way too cute."

She nudged Julia, who smiled at Cassie, who turned to B.J., poised to poke her. But Julia growled low in her throat, and Cassie retracted her poking finger.

"B.J.," Anne-Stuart said, "aren't you supposed to be working on your own project?"

Julia tossed her head. "Eddie's over there waiting for you."

Sophie looked in the direction Julia's hair had moved. Eddie Wornom was slumped in a desk in the back of the room behind a big propped-up book that said *Leonardo da Vinci* on the cover. Even though Eddie wasn't a Fruit Loop anymore, Sophie still couldn't get used to him being a decent human being.

Evidently B.J. couldn't either, because every day the Pops had to chase her off to work with him. Sophie certainly had plenty of time to watch that going on, since all she did during rehearsals was duck behind furniture and bring "Leona" cups of tea that she never drank. It was hard to get into that.

And that was very strange for Sophie. This far into the making of a film, she usually spent more time being her character than being herself. But when she tried to put on Johanna Van Raggs, she just didn't fit.

That afternoon at home, Sophie slipped into character a little in the laundry room when she had folding duty. . . . *Johanna held David Teniers's clean shirt to her face and cried into it. Would her kidnapped master ever be returned? She scowled through her tears. Not if that ridiculous Leona Artalini had anything to do with it. She didn't know as much about* The Surgeon *as Johanna herself did. Johanna clutched the shirt in her fists. If that ignorant woman demanded one more cup of tea, she was very likely to rip her in half. . . .*

"Hey!" Zeke said. "That's my best Spider-Man shirt! You tore it! Da-ad!"

The chunk that replacing Zeke's shirt took out of Sophie's saved-up allowance wasn't the worst of it. Mama and Daddy called her up to the bedroom for a sit-down-and-talk. Daddy did most of the talking.

"Your mother says you're having some issues with your Flakes, Soph," Daddy said, motioning for her to perch on the edge of the bed. "Does that have anything to do with your tearing a hole in your brother's shirt?"

Sophie could see the corners of Daddy's lips twitching like he was pinching back a smile, and she didn't appreciate it. This so wasn't funny.

"Better one of his than one of your friends'," Daddy said. "Seeing how he has enough of them to open a Spider-Man boutique." He tilted his big squarish head at her. "How am I doing so far?"

"You're close," Sophie said. "Except I didn't want to tear one of their shirts. I wanted to tear one of them. Well, Fiona."

Daddy lost control of his lips and grinned. "We can always count on you to be honest, Soph."

Mama ran her hand down Sophie's back. "Have things gotten worse?"

Sophie nodded. Somehow their niceness was making that lumpy thing in her throat bigger.

"Worse, as in it's affecting your schoolwork?" Daddy asked.

"Not yet," Sophie said. "But it could happen."

"You starting to daydream in class again?"

"No! That's just it." Sophie could hear her voice pip-squeaking. "I can't even get into my character to feel better."

Daddy ran his hand down the back of his head. "I can't believe I'm saying this, but that is cause for concern."

He and Mama looked at each other and had one of those parent conversations where no words were spoken, but things were said with their eyes.

Daddy put his big hand on the back of Sophie's neck. "You could talk to Dr. Peter about it at Bible study maybe." Sophie twisted to look at him. Her mother and father had also worked with Dr. Peter, and Daddy especially had become like a whole other parent. For months now they'd been handling things as a family.

"You think I'm that bad?" Sophie said.

"No!" they both said as if they'd been poked with the same pin.

"You're not 'bad' at all, Dream Girl," Mama said.

"You've really been a team player," Daddy said. "But with everything that's going on around here, we just thought you might like a little special coaching, that's all."

Sophie pictured herself sitting on the window seat in Dr. Peter's office, swinging her legs, and holding on to the face pillow that matched her mood.

"Okay," Sophie said. "Maybe I'll ask him about it at Bible study."

But she wasn't sure even Dr. Peter could tell her how she was supposed to feel.

Sophie said no to having sessions with her beloved Dr. Peter because *it*

5

seemed like she would be going backward. But she didn't stop dumping everything on Jesus every night.

They just aren't figuring it out yet, she told him, *even though the script is lame and the main part is too much for Fiona.*

His eyes didn't look so kind to her. *Why would they?* she thought. He was probably as mad at them as she was.

About a week into rehearsals, during sixth period, the group tried to practice the scene where Fiona was supposed to discover the final clue.

Sophie — Johanna — sat on a stool that would barely have been big enough for Zeke and watched Leona turn from the poster of *The Surgeon* and say, "Eureka!"

Sophie was supposed to get up and do a little happy-dance, which she personally thought made her look like she had to go to the bathroom. Just as she stood up, Vincent barked out, "Cut!"

"Do you have to scream?" Cassie said from just a few feet away. She waved a Magic Marker at Vincent. "You made me mess up — again."

Vincent ignored her and folded his lanky arms. It occurred to Sophie that he could have folded them over one more time and still had some arm left over.

"Fiona," he said.

"It's Leona," Maggie said.

"You're supposed to act like it's a big deal."

"I said, 'Eureka,'" Fiona said. She looked at Maggie. "Isn't that my line?"

"'Eureka,'" Maggie read from the script. "'Leona throws her arms out wide. Johanna Van Raggs does a celebration dance.'"

"You didn't throw your arms out," Vincent said.

"It looks stupid." Fiona flapped her hands like a limp bird.

"That does look stupid," Maggie said.

"So do something else to look excited," Jimmy said.

Fiona put her hands on her hips.

"No, that's not it," Vincent said.

"I know!" Sophie could tell Fiona was about to spew out her longest vocabulary words any minute now. "The point is, Leona Artalini wouldn't freak out. She's a sophisticated professional. Her reaction would be more — subtle."

"Define subtle," Darbie said.

"It's like keeping your feelings inside and just giving little clues."

"Okay, so do that," Vincent said.

Fiona turned to the poster and raised an eyebrow. "Like that," she said.

"I didn't see anything," Willoughby said. "I mean, no offense."

Fiona rolled her eyes. "The camera will just have to come in close to catch it."

Vincent shook his head. "I don't think anybody's gonna get it. Just try it the way I told you."

"You'll be fabulous, Fiona!" Willoughby said, flapping everything including her curls.

"Yeah," Vincent said. "Do it like she just did."

It was all Sophie could do not to roll *her* eyes. No famous art expert in the baroque period would act like she was cheering at a middle school basketball game.

But nobody's asking me, she thought.

"Go for it," Vincent said. "Your line before that is — "

"I know my line." Fiona snapped him a look and took her place in front of the "painting." Sophie/Johanna hunched down on the stool again, toes pointed inward, and pretended to be blown away by Leona's intelligence.

"I have searched every inch of this painting," Fiona/Leona said. Or at least that was what Sophie thought she said. She was mumbling like she was having a conversation with herself.

"But still something eludes me." Fiona leaned about an eighth of an inch closer to the poster. "Aha. It is here, up in this corner. Eureka." She stuck both arms out, scarecrow-fashion, and turned around in a circle.

Kitty gave a nervous giggle. Behind Sophie, Julia, Cassie, and Anne-Stuart fell over each other like a trio of gibbon apes.

"I don't think that was it exactly," Jimmy said.

"It didn't even come close," Vincent said.

"Unless she was trying out for the *Wizard of Oz*," Sophie heard Julia whisper to her gasping friends.

Fiona punched her hands onto her hips so hard Sophie was afraid she'd bruised herself. "I told you it would look stupid," she said.

Her voice had an angry edge, but Sophie knew better. What they were hearing was Frustrated Fiona. Clenched teeth would have been next if the bell hadn't rung.

Fiona snatched up her backpack and made for the door. Willoughby and Kitty took off after her, but Sophie knew the best thing to do was to leave her alone for a while. Frustrated Fiona had been known to throw things.

Besides, although the snickers from the Corn Pops and the scarecrow imitations from the Fruit Loops made Sophie cringe for Fiona, she couldn't quite bring herself to feel totally sorry for her.

"She'll be better tomorrow," Jimmy said to Vincent.

"She wasn't any better today than she was yesterday," Vincent said.

"Do you want me to write that down?" Maggie said.

"No," Darbie told her. She looked at Sophie. "Maybe you should talk to her."

"I'll handle it," Vincent said, almost before Darbie got the words out. "I'm the director."

He puffed out his chest, or at least he tried to. To Sophie, it was more like an attempt to inflate a shriveled-up party balloon.

That afternoon Mama's eyebrows puckered when Sophie took celery sticks and peanut butter to her room for snack-and-chat.

"Your face tells me things aren't better," Mama said.

Sophie sagged onto the bed with the plate. "They're worse."

When she'd told Mama the latest episode, she stuffed a peanut-butter-gooed piece of celery into her mouth. Mama just toyed with one.

"There's one thing I'm not hearing, Dream Girl," she said.

"What?"

"I'm not hearing that you've tried talking to any of the girls about this, especially Fiona." She tapped at the peanut butter with the tip of her finger. "I thought it was part of your Corn Flake Code to always talk things out."

"It's like I'm not even there, though," Sophie said. The throat lump got lumpier. "They're basically ignoring me."

"It would be pretty hard to ignore you on the phone," Mama said. "Maybe after you finish your homework, you could give Fiona a call?"

"Maybe," Sophie said.

But even after she'd done her homework on the computer in the family room, she couldn't imagine what she was going to say to Fiona. At least, not as Sophie...

Johanna Van Raggs retreated to her stool near the hearth and frowned into the pitiful little fire she'd built. She wished she could let Leona know what she really thought of her. "You think you know all there is to know about everything," she would tell her. "I know a lot of things that would help you in your search if you would just ask me. But no—you've made it so I can't even speak—and even if I could, you wouldn't listen because you think I'm just a stupid servant." Johanna jabbed at the fire with her poker and watched the sparks scatter fearfully for their lives. If only she could stir up Leona Da-Know-It-All that way....

"Phone for you, Soph," Lacie said. She took the fireplace poker out of Sophie's hand. "You better not let Daddy catch you playing in the fire."

She handed Sophie the phone. Sophie could hear Fiona telling her little brother and sister to "exit, stage right" so she could talk in private.

"Fiona?" Sophie said.

"Soph—I am *so* glad you're there." She didn't sound like Frustrated Fiona. In fact, her voice was a little feeble, like she'd had the flu for a couple of days. Sophie felt a flicker of hope.

"Can I ask you something, Soph?" Fiona said.

Ah. She was finally coming around.

"Ask me anything," Sophie said. She cozied up to the fire.

"Don't you think Vincent is wrong about Leona Artalini? I mean, do you really think she should be acting like one of those people on TV when they win the lottery?"

"No way," Sophie said. She was starting to glow. Mama *had* been right.

"It works for *your* character because you're, like, this uneducated peasant. But I have the lead role — *I* shouldn't be acting like I have a mental disorder."

"Well, yeah," Sophie said, squirming a little, "but — "

"And the other thing is, Vincent shouldn't have let the Pops stand there and laugh at me. I mean, I know we're not supposed to care what they think, but, hel-*lo*, rude!"

"Definitely," Sophie said. "I think — "

"I'm using Corn Flake Code on this, Soph. I'm gonna go to Vincent and just tell him that. You know, like, not in a mean way, but just say it. And I'm telling him you think the same way I do."

Sophie hitched herself closer to the fire and picked her words carefully. "You want to know what else I think?" she said.

Fiona sent her husky laugh into the phone. "I already know what you think, Soph. I always know what you think." Sophie could almost see Fiona happily rolling her eyes. "We're best friends, remember? I knew I'd feel better after I talked to you."

Fiona had to go then, and Sophie sat staring at the flames that teased her like tongues. Mama had said to try talking to Fiona.

"I did," Sophie said out loud. "But Fiona didn't try listening."

Film Club met in Miss Imes' room during lunch the next day, and Kitty was giggling so much she couldn't even eat whatever her mom had put in her Tupperware container.

"Why are you flipping out?" Vincent said to her.

"Maggie has the costume drawings! I can't wait to see what I get to wear!"

Willoughby out-poodled her loudest shriek on record, even though she wasn't getting a costume. Sophie even felt a tingle. Costumes were one of the best-best-best parts of doing a movie, especially the way Maggie's mom, Senora LaQuita, made them.

It doesn't matter if I do just stand around, Sophie thought. *At least I get to wear something period and amazing.*

They all leaned forward as Maggie propped an oversized sketchbook on Miss Imes' desk and turned to the first page.

"This is Jimmy's," Maggie said.

Kitty and Willoughby went off the scale with giggles, and Vincent grinned at Jimmy. "Dude," he said, "she did put you in tights."

Jimmy grinned back. "I wear stuff like that for gymnastics all the time."

"I heard real men can wear tights — or something like that," Nathan said. And then he skipped red and went straight to magenta.

Sophie gazed at the black billowy sleeves and the flowing cape in the drawing. If a boy's costume was this elegant, she could only imagine what the girls' would be like.

She wasn't disappointed when she saw Fiona's. Leona Artalini was to be clad in blue brocade with enough tucks and loops and puffs to upholster a roomful of furniture.

"You are going to look *fabulous*!" Willoughby said.

And so was Kitty. Her painter's outfit had green velvet breeches, a white silky shirt, and a beret with an ostrich feather that was almost bigger than Kitty herself. Sophie saw tears in Kitty's eyes as she reached out and touched the drawing. She hadn't been in a movie in so long. Sophie could almost feel Kitty's happy warmth in her own chest.

"This is for Johanna Van Raggs," Maggie said.

She flipped to the last drawing, and Sophie's warm place turned to ice.

Except for the clunky boots, everything else in the picture looked like it had been pulled from a bag of rags. The sleeves were smudgy and had gaping holes in them. The skirt was a collection of tattered strips. And the vest was laced up with a filthy piece of rope.

"Nice," Vincent said.

"That wouldn't be the word I would use to describe it," Fiona said. She tilted her head back and forth. "But it works."

"Yeah, it fits," Jimmy said. "Johanna Van Raggs in rags."

Willoughby half yelped, "Sophie, you'll look — "

"I will *not* look fabulous," Sophie said. "So don't even go there."

She barely recognized her own voice. It sounded squeezed-in, just the way she felt.

"It's definitely not fabulous," Fiona said, "but — "

Sophie didn't wait to hear the rest. She fled the scene.

6

into Darbie — whose chin was practically dragging onto her chest. For the moment, Sophie's image of herself in a moth-eaten dress dissolved.

"What's wrong, Darb?" she said.

Darbie sank against the bank of lockers and jabbed her hair behind her ears like it had better not even think about creeping back out.

"You never told me Round Table was going to be like this," she said.

"Like what?"

"Like we have to do individual peer counseling."

"We never did that," Sophie said. It immediately sounded fascinating to her. There were lots of possibilities for a dream character who didn't look like somebody's flea-bitten bag.

"Guess who Mrs. Clayton assigned me to?" Darbie said.

"Not one of the — "

"The worst. B.J. Schneider."

Sophie couldn't think of a thing to do except squeeze Darbie's hand in sympathy. This really was heinous. As much as she missed Round Table, she wouldn't want to do this.

"B.J.'s making a bags of her whole life," Darbie said. "She's already gotten two tardies in just about every class, and she's used three bathroom passes."

"Yikes."

"It gets worse. Yesterday she got caught going to the Mini-Mart during lunch."

"What was she thinking?"

"She doesn't think." Darbie tucked her hair back tighter. "And I guess I'm supposed to teach her how."

Darbie peeled herself away from the lockers and twirled the lock on her own. Sophie leaned in, facing her. "Did Mrs. Clayton and Coach Nanini tell you there's always a reason why somebody acts out?"

Darbie grunted into her locker.

"Seriously," Sophie said. "We learned that if we could figure out why a kid was acting like a moron, we could usually help them."

Darbie pulled out her science book like it was B.J.'s head and slammed the door. "I know why she's being an eejit," she said. "Because she is one."

Sophie couldn't argue with that. B.J. never had appeared to have much sense.

In fact, during sixth period that very day, while Vincent was making Fiona say, "Eureka!" every way possible, Sophie watched B.J. plop herself down in the middle of the Corn Pops and Fruit Loops and be banished to Eddie Wornom's corner for the hundredth time.

You'd think she'd get it eventually, Sophie thought. It wasn't like B.J. didn't know that when Julia decided somebody was suddenly de-Popped, that was *it* until she changed her mind. The harder B.J. tried to get back into the group, the farther Julia's lip curled, until by now it was halfway up her nose. It was a clear signal for Anne-Stuart to do her dirty work for her.

"B.J., are you, like, retarded or something?" Anne-Stuart said. She put her face close to B.J.'s and formed her words like her mouth was made of rubber. "You — are — not — in — our — project — group."

Cassie joined in. "Go — work — with — Eddie."

Tod cast a black look toward the corner where Eddie was still reading the da Vinci book. "The loser," he said.

Huh, Sophie thought. *Just because Eddie won't do the kind of heinous stuff you do anymore?*

"Oh, he's definitely a loser," Julia said. She made a huge production out of redoing her ponytail and then flipped it at B.J. "And anybody who works with him is a loser too."

"I can't help it if I ended up having to work with him!" B.J. said. "You wouldn't let me be in your group!"

Sophie had never heard B.J. that close to tears before. She almost felt sorry for her.

Anne-Stuart sniffed. Cassie snorted. Sophie was surprised Colton didn't just out and out hang a loogie. Julia parked her hand under her chin and looked at B.J.

"You know what you have to do," she said, "if you want back in the group."

"I can't," B.J. said, in a voice Sophie could barely hear.

"Then I guess you're not much of a friend." Julia raised her brows at Cassie and Anne-Stuart, who both shook their heads.

Sophie watched B.J. slink toward Eddie and da Vinci, and then she looked for Darbie. This was definitely something she needed to know if she was going to be able to help B.J. with her eejit issues for Round Table.

Fiona was on something like take 454. Fiddling with the camera, Darbie's eyes drooped as if she were about to drift off to sleep.

"We could be here for decades," Darbie murmured when Sophie perched on the desktop where Darbie was set up.

"I think we already have been," Sophie murmured back. "I have something to tell you about Round Table."

"Do you sit on the tables in your home, Sophie?"

Sophie looked up at Mr. DiLoretto. He squinted at her through his rimless glasses, sort of like a fish peering out of its bowl. Sophie slid off the desk and hoped the paper he was holding wasn't a detention slip for her.

He handed it to Darbie and softened his face into a smile.

"Something for you about Round Table," he said. "It's an honor to be on that council."

Darbie's always-white face suddenly looked sunburned. "I've only been on it for — "

"You're a girl of many talents. I like to see a student who's well rounded."

Mr. DiLoretto sliced a look at Sophie that indicated desktop-sitting, feet-tangling urchins like her didn't qualify as "well rounded."

I used to be on the Round Table! Sophie wanted to shout at him as he turned to go. *I practically started it!*

Mr. DiLoretto paused, and for a heart-stopping moment, Sophie thought she might have said it out loud.

"I suggest you start doing some work on this project," he said to her. "So far, I haven't seen you do much."

Before Sophie could decide how she was going to keep from exploding, he moved on to the Pops-Loops group.

Darbie looked up from the paper. "Did you want to tell me something, Soph?" she said.

Sophie clamped her teeth together and shook her head. "Never mind," she managed to say. "It was nothing."

Sophie decided it was a good thing they had Bible study with Dr. Peter that day after school. Without his twinkly grin to look forward to, she was sure she *would* blow up into confetti. Especially in the car on the way to the church.

Fiona's grandfather Boppa drove the Flakes in the Buntings' big Ford Expedition. Fiona was in the front seat, turned around and up on her knees so she could address the girls in the next two seats, her seat belt fastened over her rump.

"Okay," she said, "so I got really tired of Vincent telling me how to act. I even talked to him about it, but it didn't do any good."

"He's the director," Maggie said in her thud-voice. "He's supposed to tell you how to act."

Fiona twisted her little bow of a mouth into a knot. Sophie knew that look. That was Fiona trying way hard not to say something she was going to have to apologize for later. Sophie couldn't help rescuing her. Fiona was still her best friend, even if she *was* clueless.

"It's not exactly working out for you, is it?" Sophie said.

The whole car seemed to breathe a giant sigh of relief, even bald-headed Boppa.

"No," Fiona said. She beamed at Sophie. "But I think I've found the solution."

Sophie closed her eyes and tried not to grin too big. Finally, Fiona had figured it out. At this point, it wouldn't be hard for Fiona to play Johanna Van Raggs, since there were no lines. And Sophie knew all of Leona Artalini's, although the first thing she was going to do as director was change that name.

"I looked up acting on the Internet," Fiona said, "and I found this totally cool thing called 'method acting.'"

Maggie reached for her backpack. "Should I be taking notes?"

"No, it's simple. You try to become your character, not just when you're rehearsing, but, like, all the time."

Kitty blinked her china-blue eyes at Sophie. "You always do that."

"No, no," Fiona said, swatting that aside with her hand as if it were a mosquito. "You don't just pretend. You actually become it. Like, Leona's Italian, so from now until we're finished filming, I'm only going to eat pasta."

"This should be interesting," Boppa said. Sophie saw his caterpillar eyebrows wiggle in the rearview mirror. "I think we're having Chinese tonight."

Willoughby let out a little yip she'd obviously been holding back. Sophie wasn't having as much luck with her disappointment. She was sure it was smeared all over her face.

"So let me get this straight," Darbie said from the rear seat. "You and Sophie and Kitty are going to act like your characters all the time? Even in school?"

"I can't be stuffed in a closet in Miss Imes' room," Kitty said. Sophie hadn't heard her voice wind up into a whine like that in a long time. "I'll get detention!"

"I'm sure that isn't what Fiona means." Boppa glanced at his granddaughter. "It isn't, is it?"

"No — hel-*lo*!"

Fiona rolled her eyes almost up into her head. Sophie used to think it was funny when she did that. Now it crawled right up between her shoulder blades.

"You just act the way your character would act in any situation you're in," Fiona said, like she was talking to her little sister. "Wherever you are, you do what David Teniers the Younger would do."

"I don't get it," Kitty whined.

Fiona reached into the second seat and patted Kitty's hand. "Don't worry about it. Just watch Sophie and me, and you'll catch on."

When did I agree to this? Sophie thought. It was time to say something.

But as they climbed out of the car at the church, Fiona said, "Remember, you can't speak unless you absolutely have to."

Sophie stared at her.

You sure aren't going to let me forget, Sophie thought as she followed Fiona into the Bible study room. She was again ready to explode.

Each of the girls, including Harley and Gillian, their two sporty friends, the Wheaties, had a different-colored beanbag chair with a Bible in a cover to match. Sophie sank into her purple one, certain that right now her face matched it.

Fiona poked it with her toe. "Uh, Soph," she said, "you really ought to sit behind Kitty. You *are* the servant."

"I always sit here!" Sophie said.

"Shh! You're mute!"

"What gives, ladies?"

Sophie had never been so glad to see Dr. Peter. He plopped his small-for-a-man self into his own beanbag, facing them, and wrinkled his nose so that his wire-rimmed glasses scooted up. Behind them his blue eyes got their twinkly look.

"Fiona wants us to do this thing," Sophie started to say.

But once again Fiona *shhh*ed her, this time spraying her down the arm. It felt like Anne-Stuart was in the room.

"Okay, dish," Dr. Peter said. "I need details."

He folded his hands behind his crispy gelled curls, elbows sticking out, and leaned back while Fiona told him all about their roles in the movie, and how method acting was going to make them all fabulous. When she was finished, Dr. Peter gave a familiar "Ah," and Sophie let herself breathe. If she knew Dr. Peter, Fiona was about to get straightened out.

"I think I have just the story for this situation," he said. "Grab your Bibles, ladies."

Sophie wished that for once Dr. Peter would just tell Fiona she was getting carried away instead of making them figure it out. But she did like the way he always took them through the Jesus stories, just like they were actually in them.

At least I get to pick who I want to be, Sophie thought. She sneaked a glare at Fiona.

"The Gospel of Matthew, chapter 20," Dr. Peter said. "We're going to start at verse 25, but let me give you a little background first."

He told them that Jesus had just filled his disciples in on what was going to happen to him, that he was going to be crucified, but that he would rise to life again.

"And just like a bunch of guys," Dr. Peter said, "they started arguing about who were going to be Jesus' main men in his new kingdom."

"Kind of like Anne-Stuart and B.J. fighting over Julia!" Willoughby said. Then she yelped and added, "Only Julia isn't Jesus, of course."

"You've got the idea, Will," Dr. Peter said. "Anyway, here's what Jesus said to them. Imagine that you're one of Jesus' disciples."

Sophie closed her eyes and mentally put on sandals and robe and inched along to get closer to Jesus, scuffing up dust along the way. She never wanted to miss a word the Master said.

"Sophie," Darbie whispered, "you just pushed your beanbag onto my foot."

"Sorry," Sophie said without opening her eyes.

"Shhh!" Fiona said.

Sophie/Disciple craned her neck toward Jesus and tried to concentrate. Sometimes that was hard when *other* disciples annoyed her like pieces of sand between her toes.

"This is Jesus talking to you," Dr. Peter said. He read, "'You know that the rulers of the Gentiles lord it over them, and their high officials exercise authority over them.'"

Sophie/Disciple nodded at Jesus. Just the other day she'd seen somebody get thrown in jail for owing only a couple of dollars —

"'Not so with you. Instead, whoever wants to become great among you must be your servant, and whoever wants to be first must be your slave.'"

Sophie let the disciple fade as she clung to one word. Had he just said *servant*? Whoever wants to become great must be a *servant*?

"'Just as the Son of Man did not come to be served, but to serve.'"

Sophie was waving her hand before Dr. Peter even got his Bible closed. "So being a servant is a great thing?" she said.

Fiona started to shower her with yet another shushing, but Dr. Peter shook his head at her.

"Serving is a most *excellent* thing," he said to Sophie. And then his eyes swept over the group. "Does everybody get what he's saying?"

No! Sophie thought as everyone else bobbed their heads up and down. *I do NOT get that other people have the right to turn me into a nothing! What's so excellent about that?*

She slapped the Bible closed. Dr. Peter raised his eyebrows above his glasses; Sophie pretended to dig for something in her backpack.

If I'm supposed to be a servant, she thought as she clawed through her books, *then I will be SUPER Servant. Every one of them is gonna be so majorly impressed.*

Just wait 'til they saw Johanna Van Raggs tomorrow. They wouldn't dare ignore Sophie then.

When Sophie gave Mama a good-night hug that night, she assured her
that things were definitely looking better.

"So Dr. Peter did his thing, huh?" Mama said.

"In a major way," Sophie said.

"I thank God for him every day."

Sophie did that too. Snuggled into bed, she closed her eyes and
imagined him and told him he was amazing about
twelve times.

*Thank you for showing me that I have to
play the best servant I possibly can,* she said
to him. *That's how Fiona and Vincent and
everybody are gonna see who's great.*

Jesus' eyes suddenly didn't look so
kind to her. They weren't angry. They
just flashed a little in her mind.

Am I being conceited? she prayed. *I don't mean to be — but don't they have to see that they're being totally unfair to me? Now Mr. DiLoretto thinks I'm a slacker, and the movie is, like, so bad right now it's embarrassing.*

Besides all that, it wasn't fun being around Fiona anymore. Fiona was — what did the Bible say? — "lording it over her."

But not so with me, she assured Jesus, just before his eyes faded from view altogether.

Johanna Van Raggs shivered into the pile of straw she'd formed into a bed before the fire. With her wonderful master, David Teniers the Younger, being held captive somewhere, there was no one to protect her from Leona Artalini the Bossy. But she had to be the greatest servant she could be — even if she couldn't talk.

In fact, she just might be able to use that to her advantage.

When the Flakes all met at their lockers the next morning, Sophie smiled until her face hurt as she motioned for Kitty to allow her to open her stubborn lock for her. Then she insisted with sign language that Fiona let her carry her backpack to first period.

"You're acting weird, Sophie," Maggie said.

"No, she isn't," Fiona said. "She's practicing method acting."

"I still don't know how!" Kitty said tearfully.

"Just — draw something," Fiona said.

Sophie pulled her colored pencils out of her backpack and handed them to Kitty.

"Sophie's into it," Willoughby said to Kitty and Maggie as the three of them went off to their class.

Fiona snapped her fingers in the air. "Come along, Johanna. I'm going to need you to wipe off my desk before I sit in it."

"You're off your nut, Fiona," Darbie said.

But Sophie just smiled. If Darbie was getting annoyed with Fiona, then this was working already.

One of the most surprising things about being a mute servant, Sophie found out that day, was how much she heard that she usually didn't.

It was incredible to discover, for instance, that most people never stopped talking, even when they were doing their class assignments. She picked up everything from the details of the Pops' last sleepover — which she decided she would have been better off not knowing — to Mrs. Clayton and Miss Hess' whispered conversation about what a pain in the neck the new restroom log was.

She also learned that maintenance people muttered to themselves when they were picking up trash, and the ladies behind the counter in the lunch line had private nicknames for some of the students — like Bottomless Pit and Stick Girl. Miss Imes hummed a lot, and Mr. Benchley had squeaky shoes.

But it was during lunch that she made her most revealing discovery.

A lot of people from Mr. DiLoretto's class were putting in extra time on their projects in his room. Film Club had finally moved on from the "eureka" scene, and Vincent was explaining how he wanted Fiona to pry open the secret door into the villain artist's dungeon where Kitty/David was being held.

"Pretend this is a crowbar," he said. He handed her a ruler. "We'll get a real one when we film this weekend."

Fiona shook her head. "Leona wouldn't use a crowbar."

"Why?" Vincent said.

"Because it doesn't feel right for my character." She turned her face so Sophie could wipe her forehead.

"Who cares how it feels? How else is she supposed to get in?"

"She'd use something clever — "

Sophie tugged at Fiona's sleeve and handed her a letter opener from the prop box.

"Maybe a letter opener," Fiona said.

"You guys," Jimmy said, pulling off his villain's mask. "Could we just practice the scene the way it is so we can get through this?"

Fiona sniffed. "I'm just exercising my creative rights."

"You're just exercising your mouth," Vincent muttered.

Sophie saw that she was the only one who'd heard him. Everyone else was debating the crowbar versus the letter opener.

"Use *this*!" Vincent said, and he slapped the ruler onto the table. It snapped neatly in half.

"Beautiful," Fiona said. She looked at Sophie. "Johanna, fix this."

"Rude to her," Maggie said flatly.

Darbie grunted. "It's that methodical acting thing or whatever it is."

Willoughby dug some nail glue out of her backpack, and Sophie sat in a desk in the back of the room and went to work on the broken "crowbar."

"What smells?" Anne-Stuart said, wrinkling her nose.

"Oh," Cassie said, "it's Sophie."

"Ha-ha," a male voice said. It was Eddie, slumped behind da Vinci in the row next to Sophie, sounding anything but amused.

"Yeah, they really think they're funny."

That came from B.J., who was actually sitting by him. Sophie was so surprised, she let the ruler clatter to the desktop and break apart again. She left it there and started over with the glue, but she kept her ears perked up to Eddie and B.J. Something was, as Johanna Van Raggs herself would say, amiss.

"*You* think they're funny," Eddie said to B.J.

"I used to. Not anymore."

Eddie grunted. "Not since they dumped you."

"They didn't dump me — I dumped them."

That is such a lie! Sophie thought. She furrowed her forehead over the gluing project and listened harder.

"Whatever," Eddie said. "Then why do you spend more time over there than you do helping me figure out what we're gonna do for this project? We don't even have an idea yet."

"I was spying on them," B.J. said.

Eddie paused. Sophie wanted to look to see what kind of expression he had on his face, but she just had to imagine it. She decided on being cautiously suspicious.

"Why?" Eddie said finally.

"So I could find out what they're doing, and then we can do the same thing only do it three times better and make them look stupid."

"I don't wanna do that," Eddie said.

"Do you 'wanna' get an F?"

Eddie's silence said he didn't. Sophie clutched the desk with her hands so she wouldn't jump up and yell, "Don't do it, Eddie! She's lying!"

"It's not like we'd be cheating," B.J. said. "It would be our own work."

There was another deciding pause. Sophie held on harder to the desktop.

"If I show them down," Eddie said finally, "they'll hate me worse than ever. I already got them busted last semester."

"No," B.J. said, "they can't hate you any worse than they already do."

"Thanks," Eddie said. "That really makes me feel better."

You don't want people like that liking you, Sophie wanted to say to him. She almost wished Film Club had invited him to work with them.

"Sophie, I want to talk to you."

Sophie jerked her head up toward Mr. DiLoretto, who was standing over her.

"I'm working, honest," she said. "I'm fixing a prop."

His eyes went to B.J. and Eddie, who were suddenly quiet. If they hadn't noticed her sitting there before, they definitely did now.

"Let's step out into the hall," Mr. DiLoretto said to Sophie.

She nodded and slid sideways to get out of the desk. Her hands wouldn't go with her.

She could feel her eyes bulging as she tugged first one hand and then the other. Both of them were stuck hard to the desktop, and they weren't moving.

This couldn't be happening again.

Biting her lip against the pain, Sophie gave her hands another yank, but all she got was the taste of blood on her tongue.

"What seems to be the problem?" Mr. DiLoretto said. His voice was edging toward disaster, just like last time.

"I was putting the crowbar back together," Sophie said. She swallowed the throat-lump, which was now the size of a dumpling.

"Tell me you did *not* glue yourself to that desk."

"Not on purpose!"

One look at his twisted face, and Sophie knew he wasn't buying it. Neither was anybody else who gathered around.

"She's stuck?" Cassie said.

"Ooh, Freak Show," Colton said. He and Tod high-fived each other, while the Pops rolled their eyes in unison.

"She just gets weirder by the minute, doesn't she, Julia?" B.J. said. She threw her head back and laughed too loud.

Julia squinted her face at her.

"You want me to try pulling her loose?" Eddie asked.

"No!" said all the Flakes in unison.

"All right, quiet!"

The crowd muffled its laughter. Mr. DiLoretto looked as if he were trying to control a riot.

"Whose glue was this?" he said.

"Mine," Willoughby said in a tiny voice. "I use it for my fake nails."

"Do you have any remover?"

Sophie just knew the answer was going to be no.

"What about you, Julia?" Fiona said.

"Are you kidding?" Julia tossed her hair. "My nails are real."

"Could somebody just get me unstuck?" Sophie said. Her voice squeaked; the Loops laughed, but she didn't care. A panicky feeling filled her chest. It was like being trapped in an elevator.

The bell rang, and the kids currently gaping at Sophie went reluctantly to fifth period.

"I'll stay with you, Soph," Fiona said.

"I won't write you a pass," Mr. DiLoretto said. He glared at Fiona as if she had personally glued Sophie's hands down herself.

"Call me later," Fiona said as she walked backward out of the room. "I'm leaving this period to go to the dentist. I'm sorry — "

"I'll be okay," Sophie said to her. But she wasn't sure about that, especially when one of the muttering maintenance men arrived with a large bottle of something that smelled like a beauty salon — and a real crowbar.

Mr. DiLoretto's fifth-period class was already filing in when Sophie's hands finally came loose, without the help of the crowbar.

"You've got acetone on you," Mr. Maintenance muttered. "Better go wash it off."

"May I have a pass?" Sophie said to Mr. DiLoretto.

"You're kidding, right?" he said.

He did write her one, although he seemed to take a great deal of glee in entering it into his computer.

Even though she was already late to Mr. Stires' class, Sophie hurried to the restroom. Maybe if she was only a couple of minutes after the bell, he would take pity on her.

She burst into the restroom, headed for a sink, and found B.J. leaning over one, shoulders shaking.

At first, Sophie thought she was laughing.

Come on, Sophie wanted to say to her. *It wasn't that funny. Haven't you ever seen anybody glued to a desk before?*

But as Sophie stood at the next sink and reached for the faucet, she heard B.J.'s ragged breathing. She wasn't giggling. She was sobbing.

For a second or two, Sophie considered enjoying the moment. B.J. and the Pops had driven *her* to tears more than once.

But the words *It is not so with you* rippled through her thoughts.

Sophie stepped a little closer to B.J. "Are you okay?" she asked.

"Does it look like I'm okay?" B.J. said.

"No. I guess that was kind of a lame question."

B.J. looked quickly at Sophie through a panel of her butter-blonde bob.

"Are you sick?" Sophie said.

"Yes. I just threw up, so don't go in that first stall."

"You must have eaten the hot lunch."

"No! I'm just sick of being treated like a piece of trash! They're supposed to be my friends!"

"Oh," Sophie said. "What are they mad at you for?"

"I don't know! I didn't even do anything! And now they want me to *earn* my way back in — "

B.J. stumbled over a sob. When she caught her breath again, she pushed her hair out of her face and narrowed her eyes at Sophie — which didn't take much since they were already almost swollen shut.

"I bet you're loving this, aren't you?" she said.

"Uh, no," Sophie said.

B.J. smacked at the tears on her face and stood up taller, so that she was looking down at Sophie. "If you tell anybody what I just said, I'll call you a liar."

"Who would I tell?" Sophie said.

But as she picked up her backpack and half ran to Mr. Stires' class, she knew there was one person she *should* tell.

She forgot about that, though, when she got a tardy from Mr. Stires, who looked anything but cheerful as he put it on the computer. And then the minute she walked into sixth period, Mr. DiLoretto nodded for her to join him in the hall.

I haven't been humiliated enough? she thought as she followed him. Her palms were still red and throbbing, not to mention her pride. Tod and Colton couldn't even look at her without pounding on each other like a pair of baboons.

Sophie watched Mr. DiLoretto adjust his glasses and waited for him to give her detention — or worse, tell her she had to pay to have the desk refinished. He put his hands in his pockets and jingled the contents.

"Are you ever serious at all?" he said, doubt lurking in his eyes.

"I'm serious a lot," Sophie said. "I'm serious right now."

"Can you get serious enough to give somebody in this class some acting help?"

Sophie felt her mouth drop open.

"Several people have told me you're pretty good," he said. "Including Miss Imes, Mrs. Clayton — " He shook his head, ponytail sliding back and forth. "I sure haven't seen any evidence of it. But if you want a chance to make up for the things you've pulled, you can do some individual coaching."

In spite of how little Sophie wanted to make up for anything with this person, it did feel a little bit good to be asked. It would be like directing again. As long as she didn't have to work with some Corn Pop or Fruit Loop.

"Who's the person?" Sophie said.

"Tough case," he said. "I want you to see if you can get a spark of life out of Fiona Bunting."

8

the next day. But late that afternoon, when she was watching Zeke, the other answers she could have given flipped through her head like radio stations. She put Zeke to work coloring in his new Spider-Man coloring book and listened to them all in her head.

Fiona took the leading role that always belonged to Sophie, and now she was supposed to help Fiona play it right?

She's not gonna let me help her! She thinks she knows everything about acting because she read something on the Internet.

And what if Sophie did help her? Vincent would say he was the director, even though that had always been Sophie's job too.

Sophie hung off the chair by the fireplace with her head upside down. Maybe she'd missed something in what Dr. Peter said. Being the best servant on the planet wasn't working out quite the way she'd expected.

Johanna Van Raggs picked up the broom and attacked the hearth with it. Dust and ashes flew, but she didn't care. Let Leona Artalini clean it up. Johanna wasn't HER servant anyway.

Johanna swung the broom hard across the stones. The Master, Jesus, said whoever wants to become great among them must be a servant. If that was true, she must be the greatest by now. What else had he said?

Johanna frowned as she swept harder and tried to remember. It used to be so easy to think when Mister David had been there, quietly painting in the corner. She could almost imagine him there, creating the smallest of details with his brush....

She shook her head, scolding herself. There was no time to long for him now. I must find a way to get that evil Leona — whatever her name is — to give me back my rightful place. I was never treated this way before. I don't deserve it!

She gave the hearth a resounding smack with the broom and coughed until her eyes were streaming. "I'm trying so hard to be good!" she cried. "But I feel like a slave — to everybody!"

The cottage door slammed —

Sophie jumped and dropped the broom. It fell into a layer of ashes that stretched across the hearth and onto the rug.

"What happened in *here*?" Lacie said from the family room doorway.

That wasn't the worst of it. Daddy stood next to her, only he wasn't looking at the mess on the floor. His eyes were riveted to the wall, where the *real* worst of it was happening. Zeke was putting the finishing touches on a spiderweb he'd drawn up there with a red marker.

This, Sophie decided, would be an excellent time to be the servant. Heart pounding, she started for the kitchen. "I'll clean it up," she said.

"Stop!" Lacie and Daddy said in stereo.

Sophie froze.

"You'll track it all over the house," Daddy said. "Lace, go get some—"

"I'm on it," Lacie said.

"And take Z-Boy with you."

"Sophie said it was okay!" Zeke wailed as Lacie hoisted him over her shoulder.

"No, I didn't!" Sophie said. "Daddy, I *didn't*!"

"You didn't say he couldn't. That's a yes in his mind."

Sophie put her hands on the sides of her face. "I'm sorry. I was daydreaming. I guess you figured that out."

"Sounded more like a nightmare to me," Daddy said.

"Was I saying stuff out loud?"

Daddy nodded. Sophie wished she could disappear into the ashes at her feet.

"Am I in trouble?" she asked.

Daddy's big square face got soft at the corners. "Not the kind you mean."

"What kind?"

He wiped his hand across his mouth, like he was trying to get rid of a smile. "It's a little hard to have a serious conversation when you have soot all over your face. Let's get you cleaned up, and then you and Mama and I will talk."

"About my trouble," Sophie said.

"Yeah, Baby Girl. About your trouble."

Daddy scooped her up, carried her upstairs, and deposited her in the bathroom. She would have laughed at the sight of herself in the mirror, looking like the chimney sweep in *Mary Poppins*, if she hadn't felt so confused. One thing was for sure — she wasn't going to mention this to Vincent, or he'd want her to smear ashes all over herself for the film.

Ugh. The film.

"It's the first time I ever didn't want to do a movie," she told Mama and Daddy when she was soot-free enough to sit on the edge of Mama's bed. "And it's not because I want to be the star." She bumped her legs against the mattress. "Well, that's not the only reason."

"Sounds to me like it's the way it's being handled that's got you all fired up," Daddy said. He put one hand up on the bedpost and ran the other one down the back of his head. "You know, Soph, you can't control the way other people behave." He grinned. "I mean, look at Zeke."

"That's the problem," Sophie said. "I *wasn't* looking at him."

Mama laughed her little soft laugh and rubbed Sophie's back with her toe. "It happens to the best of us. Remember the time I turned my back for two minutes, and he flushed one of his action figures down the toilet?"

"The thing is, though, Soph," Daddy said, "we're afraid you might drift off into Dreamland in school again, just when you're doing so well." He slid his arm down and sat halfway on the bed next to Mama. Sophie could look right into his eyes. "And it sounds like you're pretty ticked off at Fiona. I've never seen you — uh — vent like that before."

"Venting's healthy," Mama said. "But only if you do it with the right person."

Sophie nodded slowly. "You want me to talk to Dr. Peter, don't you?"

"Daddy and I *are* getting better at helping you sort things out," Mama said.

Daddy nodded. "But if you need something a little speedier, Dr. Peter might be your go-to guy right now."

Later, after Sophie vented again — this time to Jesus — she figured maybe they were right. She did need to talk to Dr. Peter, because even when she was imagining herself as Johanna Van Raggs, she hadn't been able to remember what else he'd told them that Jesus said. Maybe that missing piece was the reason the whole servant thing wasn't making her feel so great.

What it *was* making her was the punch line for every joke in the seventh grade. Sophie caught on to that first thing the next morning when she found glue on the handle of her locker. Fortunately she smelled it before she grabbed it.

"If I got stuck again," she told Darbie, "I'd have to change schools."

"Those eejits," Darbie said.

After that she was afraid to put her hands on anything, including the bottle she found on her desk first period that had "Glue Remover" printed on it in Sharpie. One whiff told her it wasn't glue *remover* but glue itself.

All during third-period PE, Colton and Tod pretended their hands were stuck to the basketballs, and in fourth period Miss Imes was absent so they had a sub, which was the perfect opportunity for an everybody-cough-at–10:45. Only they didn't cough. The whole class put their hands on their desktops and yelled "Ouch!" at the same time. Except for Darbie and Fiona and the Wheaties, who all assured Sophie on the way to lunch that half the people didn't even know why they were doing it.

"It's not about you, Soph," Fiona said. "It's about them being just — repugnant."

"I don't know what that means," Darbie said, "but I like it."

"It's like repulsive," Fiona said.

Darbie made a sour face. "Then it's perfect for what I have to do now."

"What?" Sophie said.

"Go to Round Table and try to work with you-know-who."

"Excellent timing."

They all stopped in front of the cafeteria and looked at Mr. DiLoretto, who was coming out with a *Phantom of the Opera* lunch box. "If Darbie can't work on your project during lunch," he said, "this is a good time for you" — he waved the lunchbox toward Sophie — "to work with Fiona."

"On what?" Fiona said.

Sophie wanted to open Mr. DiLoretto's lunch pail and crawl in.

"You haven't told her?" he said to Sophie.

"I didn't know I was supposed to."

"Oh, this is going very well so far." He turned to Fiona. "You're having a hard time with your part. I put Sophie on it."

Sophie felt Fiona stiffen beside her. "You gave her my part?" she said.

Mr. DiLoretto shook his head. "There is nothing more overly sensitive than a middle school girl. No, I asked her to coach you. You need help."

"It wasn't my idea," Sophie told Fiona as they hurried away from him toward the courtyard.

Fiona shrugged, but Sophie could tell by the way her mouth was knotting up that she was tucking her real feelings safely away. When the hurt disappeared from her eyes, she said, "Vincent's the one who needs help, not me."

"He didn't ask me to help Vincent," Sophie said. "I'm *your* servant, remember?"

Fiona hit her forehead with the heel of her hand. The sound made Sophie's own forehead hurt.

"Why did you hit yourself?" she said.

"Boppa told me people in Italy do that all the time. It means they just figured something out. And since Leona's Italian — "

"What did you just figure out?" Sophie said with a sigh. She'd given up hoping Fiona would figure out what Sophie wanted her to figure out.

"I don't know why I didn't think of it sooner," Fiona said. "Mr. DiLoretto doesn't get method acting either. That's why he thinks I need help." She stopped in front of one of the concrete benches and dropped her backpack onto it. "Did you try to explain it to him?"

Sophie felt bristly between the shoulder blades. "No. The thing is, if he doesn't think you're playing the part that well, maybe the whole method thing *isn't* working."

"Huh," Fiona said. "It's working for you. Ever since I taught it to you, Johanna Van Raggs has gotten way better."

"Yeah, but it isn't working for *you*, because Leona Artalinguini *hasn't*."

Fiona looked so stunned, Sophie thought for a second she'd hit herself in the forehead again. Then she realized she had just smacked Fiona herself, with a sentence.

"In the first place, it's Artalini," Fiona said. "And in the second place — I'm that bad, huh?"

"You really want to know?" Sophie asked.

"Hel-*lo*! Yes! I don't want to make an idiot out of myself!"

"Okay." Sophie sat on the bench and pointed the toes of her shoes toward each other. "You're playing Leona all stuck-up, and I don't think she'd be that way."

"Then how's she supposed to be?" Fiona said. "I mean, when I open my mouth, that's what comes out."

"You're the one who made her Italian," Sophie said. "So act Italian — and not, like, bring a plate of spaghetti to rehearsal."

"Duh!"

"More like—thump." Sophie thumped her own forehead with her palm. "Eureka!"

Fiona copied her. Even though it was only a halfway try, it was the best thing Sophie had seen Leona do yet.

"Do it again," Sophie said, "only bigger." It was better this time. Sophie felt herself smiling a little. "What if you said everything with an Italian accent?" she said. "You know, like we do when we're making pizza crust with Boppa."

"Really?" Fiona said one of her lines, bouncing the words up and down mama-mia style. Sophie giggled.

"It sounds stupid," Fiona said.

"No, it doesn't! Do some more. Do that scene where you're telling me to get you a cup of tea, only act it out. What else did Boppa tell you about Italians?"

"They always talk with their hands."

"So do that."

By the time the bell rang, Fiona was standing up on the bench, doing her eureka scene like an opera singer. Sophie was holding her sides so they wouldn't split from laughing.

"Was I good?" Fiona said.

"You were fabulous," Sophie said. She handed Fiona her backpack and steered her in the direction of the lockers.

"Let's do it for everybody in Film Club sixth period," Fiona said. "I think—"

They both stopped as they rounded the corner. B.J. was standing in front of her open locker, blocking their path.

"Excuse us," Fiona said.

When B.J. didn't move, Fiona said, "Hel-*lo*," but Sophie put a hand on her arm to stop her. The way B.J. was staring at her bare locker, it was obvious she didn't even know they were there.

"Where's my stuff?" B.J. said. Her voice was so shrill, Sophie winced as if someone had run a fingernail down a chalkboard. "It's all gone — all my pictures — all my *stuff*!"

B.J. grabbed the sides of her head and pulled at her hair. More things came out of her mouth, but she was screaming so far up into the atmosphere, Sophie couldn't tell what she was saying.

"It looks like somebody tore down all her decorations," Fiona whispered to Sophie, though there was no need. Sophie could barely hear her own thoughts over B.J.'s hysteria. Two girls entered the locker row from the other end, did an about-face, and ran. B.J. sank to the floor, her skirt puddling around her, and wailed.

"What's going on?" Maggie said behind Sophie.

"Somebody ripped off all her Corn Pop stuff," Fiona told her.

"Why?" Maggie said.

Sophie was pretty sure she knew why, and who. And, clearly, B.J. did too. She rocked back and forth on the floor, hitting her head against the bottom locker.

"This is getting scary," Sophie said. "I think we need a grown-up."

"I'll go," Fiona said.

"What should I do?" Maggie said, backing away from B.J.

"Maybe you should tell all those people to stop staring," Sophie said. She nodded to the crowd of gapers forming at the end of the row.

"Yeah," Maggie said. "They're all gonna be late."

She marched toward them, and Sophie squatted beside B.J.

"You shouldn't bang your head," Sophie said. "You might get brain damage or something."

She knew it was probably completely the wrong thing to say, but she couldn't just let B.J. keep it up until she knocked herself out.

"Maybe it was some stupid boy," Sophie said. "Or maybe it was somebody that's jealous because you're a — Julia's friend."

"NOOOOO!" B.J. cried. "She hates me! They all hate me! I don't know what to do without them. I'm nobody now."

"You're not nobody," Sophie said. "I mean — you're somebody."

"You don't understand — you've never been popular. My life is over!"

Sophie wasn't sure *what* she was supposed to say to that, but at least B.J. had stopped slamming herself into somebody's locker door.

"Maybe the way it used to be is over," Sophie said. "But — "

"I don't want it to *be* any other way! I have to have my Julia — and my Annie-Stew — "

"You call her 'Annie-Stew'?" Sophie said.

B.J. nodded. Some strands of her hair caught on the tears on her cheeks and plastered themselves to her face. "We all have cute nicknames." Her face crumpled. "Had."

"You'll find another Annie-Stew."

"I can't. There isn't one. I just want to die!"

"Whoa, whoa — there's no dying in the locker hall."

Sophie had never been so glad to hear the high-pitched-for-a-man voice of Coach Nanini. He squatted beside the two of them and tilted his shaved head at Sophie. "What's up, Little Bit?"

"B.J.'s friends broke up with her," Sophie said. "She's kind of upset."

"I have to get out of here!" B.J. said. "I can't stay here!"

She scrambled up and tore for the hallway. Two steps later she was sprawled out, and she stayed there, pounding the floor with her fists.

"Okay, Beej," Coach Nanini said. His words were soft. "Take it easy now...."

Sophie watched him talk down her sobs and her shouts and her flailing around. The B.J. he helped off the floor was limp and shaky, hunched over at the shoulders. Sophie had to look twice to make sure it was still her. As Coach led her away, Sophie swallowed down the lump in her throat.

Who knew I could feel so bad for a Corn Pop? Sophie thought. And then she grunted. *So bad that I forgot to ask Coach Virile for a pass.*

This was going to mean another tardy from Mr. Stires. But right then, it didn't seem like the worst thing that could happen to somebody.

9

The Corn Flakes didn't have a chance to talk again until sixth period. By

then, Darbie was fuming and shoving her hair behind her ears.

"I wasted a whole lunch period waiting for B.J., and she never showed up."

Fiona rolled her eyes. "That's because she was having a major meltdown at the lockers."

Sophie looked over at the Corn Pops. The way everybody else in the entire class was whispering, surely the Pops had heard about B.J. by now. But they were acting like one of their former best friends hadn't thrown herself on the floor an hour ago because they had rejected her. Julia was drawing a heart on the back of Tod's hand with a red Sharpie, and Anne-Stuart and Cassie were looking on as if Julia were Leonardo da Vinci himself, giving them an art lesson.

Who needs friends like that, B.J.? Sophie thought.

"So-oph, hel-*lo-o*."

Sophie looked quickly at Fiona, who said, "Let's do that scene for them."

Sophie shook B.J. out of her head and made room for Johanna Van Raggs. The rest of Film Club watched as she and Fiona acted out the eureka scene just as they'd done it in the courtyard, only better, of course, since they had an audience.

When they were finished, Willoughby did her poodle thing, Kitty clapped, and Maggie said to Darbie, "I wish you would've been filming that."

"That rocked," Jimmy said.

Nathan nodded without even turning red.

Fiona lowered her chin at Vincent. "Well?" she said.

Vincent leaned his chair onto its back legs and rubbed his chin.

Fiona slitted her eyes at him. "You irritating little man."

"Say it for me, Willoughby," Vincent said.

Willoughby squealed, "That was *fabulous*!"

Vincent parked his pencil behind his ear. "So what made you get so much better, like, overnight? Was it what I said yesterday?"

"No," Fiona said. She gave him a smug little smile.

Sophie stood up straighter and got ready to be modest. She would, of course, compliment Fiona back on taking direction so well—

"I just got the idea to do it ultra-Italian," Fiona said. "I was playing her way too conceited, you know?"

Jimmy snapped his fingers. "That's what it was. I kept thinking there was something wrong."

"I figured it out." Fiona popped her palm against her forehead, and everybody laughed.

Everybody except Sophie. All she could do was stare at Fiona.

You got the idea? You decided to play her Italian? Sophie was ready to stomp her foot through the floor. *You didn't figure it out, Fiona. I did!*

"Okay, we're on a roll," Vincent said. "Try another scene."

Darbie picked up the camera. "I'm going to film it this time. I want you to see how class you are, Fiona."

Sophie had to sit on both hands so she wouldn't reach up and snatch the camera and bonk Fiona over the head with it.

I can't believe I'm thinking that! she told herself.

But she couldn't believe Fiona was taking all the credit for her performance either. It made Sophie's neck prickle and her sight narrow down to pinpoints. Her mind darted around for a way to get back what was rightfully hers. She landed on one the minute Vincent said, "Action!"

"Maid! A cup of tea!" Fiona/Leona said.

"Cut!" Vincent said.

"What?"

"Do it with the Italian accent."

"Oh," Fiona said. "I forgot."

"Take 2."

Fiona said her line again, this time sounding like she was calling out an order at a pizza place. Sophie leaped up, curtsied several times, and bounded for the exit they'd made out of two desks. Just before she got there, she made the perfect pratfall. She heard kids all over the room laughing like they knew a good piece of slapstick when they saw it.

"Cut!" Vincent cried.

"Would you quit cutting?" Darbie said. "Just go on, would you?"

Fiona continued her lines, and Sophie waited for her entrance. Should she come in with the teacup balanced on her head, or the teaspoon tucked behind her ear the way Vincent carried his pencil?

Whatever I do, she thought, *it has to be better than what Fiona's doing.*

She decided to do both the spoon behind the ear *and* the teacup on the head, and was rewarded with appreciative guffaws from the growing number of other kids who were watching. That made it easier to come up with more things, like making faces at Fiona/Leona behind her back and imitating her every move.

When the scene was over, there was a round of applause from the rest of the class. Fiona bowed.

She thinks they're clapping for her, Sophie thought. Didn't anybody else see that she was taking all the credit for herself when she didn't even know what she was doing?

It didn't seem like it. Vincent wasn't even paying attention. He was arguing with Darbie about who was supposed to shoot from what angle. Nathan and Jimmy were laughing with the rest of the class. Maggie was bent over scowling at her script. They didn't get it.

Sophie folded her arms. Dr. Peter hadn't gotten it either. Maybe if she could make *him* see, he could help her with everybody else.

"I need to take the camera home tonight," she told Darbie.

"You can watch yourself then," Darbie said. She gave a little grunt.

"What?" Sophie said.

"Nothing," she said, although there was obviously *something*, the way she was shoving her hair. She stuck the camera in its bag and handed it to Sophie. "Wasn't Fiona just grand today?"

Thanks to me! Sophie wanted to say.

But it was okay. She could say it to Dr. Peter that very afternoon and show him the evidence.

"Sophie-Lophie-Loodle!" he said to her when she arrived at his office.

She felt her smile almost reaching her earlobes. It hadn't done that in days. When she hopped up onto the window seat where she and Dr. Peter always sat, she chose the pillow with the biggest lopsided grin and held it against herself.

"The Happy Pillow is an interesting choice, Loodle," Dr. Peter said.

"I'm just so glad to be here," Sophie said. "*You* understand, and right now it feels like everybody else on the whole planet doesn't."

He twinkled his eyes at her and inched his glasses up with a wrinkle of his nose. "I can't do anything about everybody else on the whole planet, but I can listen to *you*."

"Fabulous," Sophie said, "because I have a lot to say."

She poured out absolutely everything, from the day at the museum when Film Club had planned the whole project without her to that very afternoon when Fiona had let everybody think she had created the new Leona all by herself.

"And you know what?" Sophie said.

"No," Dr. Peter said, "but I bet I'm about to find out."

His eyes were very still, as if he'd turned off their twinkle. Sophie considered not telling him this next thing about Fiona. He was already looking disappointed enough.

"You don't think bad of Fiona because I'm telling you all this, do you?" Sophie said.

"I'm just interested in what *you* think. It's good that you're concerned for Fiona, but remember — "

"Whatever we say in here stays in here," Sophie said with him. She took a big breath. "Okay, so here's the rest of it. When we did another scene, not the one I helped her with, she went back to being terrible as Leona. I can even show you."

"I'm all over it," Dr. Peter said.

He plugged her camera into the TV on the shelf with the collection of frogs that had feeling words on them, and Sophie curled into the corner of the window seat. It was so good to be back here. It was going to be okay. It always was with Dr. Peter.

"Ready?" Dr. Peter said.

"Action!" Sophie said.

The screen flickered to life with a close-up of Fiona demanding a cup of tea in a stiff voice. The camera stayed on her with Vincent in the background yelling, "Cut!"

"I love the creative process," Dr. Peter said.

Fiona was back, calling for her tea, when suddenly something bounded across the screen, blocking Fiona and everything else with a bug-eyed face.

"That's me!" Sophie said.

"You're a little hard to miss, Loodle," Dr. Peter said.

That was definitely the truth. Through the whole scene, every time the camera settled on Fiona, laughter erupted in the background, and the camera panned dizzily to Sophie.

At least Sophie *thought* it was herself. She remembered being in the scene, but this obnoxious person couldn't be *her*. In fact, she reminded Sophie of somebody else — she just couldn't quite remember who.

Not until Fiona/Leona began to search the "room," looking for clues and chattering away like she had a mouth full of pasta. Sophie was right there, in front of her whenever possible, rolling her eyes and mocking Fiona's walk. Sophie played to the audience so that their laughter drowned out everything Fiona's character was saying.

Then she realized who that girl grabbing all the attention reminded her of. Sophie was acting just like B.J., showing off for the Corn Pops. Trying to get back what used to be hers.

"Dr. Peter?" Sophie said. "Could you turn that off?"

Dr. Peter punched the Off button like he'd been waiting for her to say the word. The obnoxious girl on the screen blipped away.

"You didn't like what you saw?" Dr. Peter asked.

"I was heinous," Sophie said. She shoved the Happy Pillow aside. "Do you have a pillow that looks like it can't stand itself?"

Dr. Peter joined her on the seat and wrinkled his glasses up his nose again. "No. You don't really want to hold on to that feeling, do you?"

"I'd rather hold a porcupine — but it's the truth!"

"Then let's get to work."

Sophie sagged against the pile of puffy ears and noses and lips. "You want to know why I was trying to steal the attention away from Fiona."

"Right."

"And you want to know because that's not who I really am."

"Uh-huh."

"Only it must be kind of who I am because I'm acting that way."

Dr. Peter nodded. "Go ahead. You're on a roll."

"Downhill!" Sophie said.

"That's okay. It's a direction."

Sophie resituated on the seat, although she couldn't find a comfortable position. "It's not because I have to be the star all the time."

"Okay."

"That's part of it — which is repulsive — but it's not because I think I know everything about acting and directing. I mean, it's repugnant enough that I think I know more than Vincent does. Only I can't help it because it's like *in* me — and they just keep taking it, and they can't do that because it's not fair! That's why I was acting like a Corn-Poppy obnoxious little brat-child!"

She had to stop to take a breath.

"Anything else?" Dr. Peter asked.

Sophie gave her head a miserable shake. "No. Is that enough?"

"Oh, I think it'll get us started."

At least his eyes were twinkling again. Sophie knew hers weren't.

He rubbed his hands together like he always did when they were about to dig into Sophie's troubles. She wished she felt as eager about it as he looked. "Okay," he said, "first of all, we need to work on the name-calling."

"Did I call somebody a name?" Sophie said.

"Yeah — one of my favorite people." He leaned forward. "You."

"Me?"

"You said you were heinous. Repulsive. Obnoxious. What was the other one?"

"Repugnant."

"That's it. You have to be careful what labels you put on yourself, Loodle, because you'll start to believe them. And basically we act out what we believe."

"I believe I'm all tangled up!"

Dr. Peter wiggled his eyebrows. "Then you've come to the right place. Shall we get out the de-tangler?"

He reached for the Bible he always kept on the shelf under the seat.

"Uh-oh," Sophie said.

"What, uh-oh?"

"That's how I got all knotted up in the first place."

"You mean the story we read in Bible study?"

She nodded as she watched him flip to Matthew 20, her stomach turning with the pages. "Jesus said if you wanted to be great you should be a servant, and I tried to be, like, this amazing Johanna Van Raggs, and it just made me a moron."

Dr. Peter blinked. "Jesus wasn't talking about a movie, Loodle."

"I know," Sophie said. "But I thought that's why you wanted me to hear it — to tell me to show Fiona and everybody that they were making a mistake. I thought I was supposed to be Super Servant in our film."

She could tell by the way he blinked at her again that that wasn't it at all. She smacked her forehead with her palm.

"Before you start bullying yourself," Dr. Peter said, "let's look at it. I think you missed something."

"I know!" Sophie said. "I keep thinking that."

Dr. Peter grinned. "Then let's go in."

He read the passage again. Sophie remembered it all, until he got to the last line.

"'Whoever wants to be first must be your slave—just as the Son of Man did not come to be served, but to serve.'"

Dr. Peter peeked over the top of the Bible at her. "How are we doing?"

"That last part, about just like Jesus didn't come to be served—"

"Yeah?"

"That's the part I missed."

"Aha! We're making progress."

Sophie suddenly felt all the stuffed noses and lips on the pillows poking into her back. "I don't think I'm serving the way Jesus did. But I still don't get it. I always thought I *was* helping people when I directed our movies."

"You were," Dr. Peter said. "A couple of them really got me thinking. But Loodle, there are a lot of different ways to serve. Seems like you're learning some of the other ones right now."

"What are they?" Sophie said.

"This could be hard to hear," Dr. Peter said.

"I'm ready," Sophie said.

Right now she didn't care if she had to spoon-feed Fiona her lunch, if it would get the knots out of her own stomach.

Dr. Peter did the hand-rubbing thing again. "The good news is, Jesus didn't give

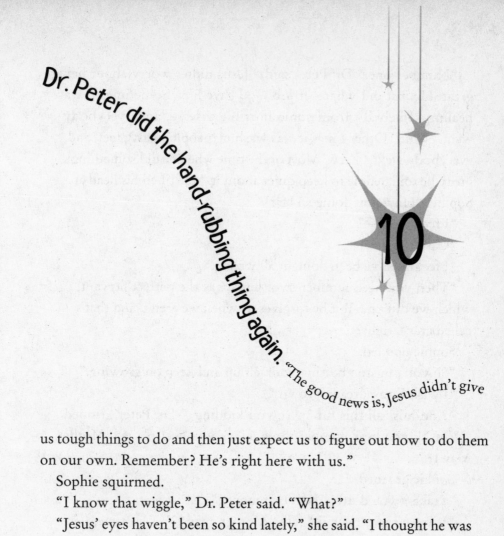

10

us tough things to do and then just expect us to figure out how to do them on our own. Remember? He's right here with us."

Sophie squirmed.

"I know that wiggle," Dr. Peter said. "What?"

"Jesus' eyes haven't been so kind lately," she said. "I thought he was disappointed in Fiona and the others, just like I was."

"Not to worry," Dr. Peter said. "He understands when we don't get it."

Sophie grabbed the cushion with the big furry eyebrows that pinched together. Anxious Pillow seemed like the only choice right now.

"Number one," Dr. Peter said. "Jesus didn't worry about being great. He just did whatever job God gave him. Sometimes it was healing somebody from some horrible disease, and everybody went, '*Wow.*' Other times it was washing people's nasty feet, and everybody went, '*Yuck.*' Most of the time when he did something great, he told people to keep quiet about it." He tilted his head at Sophie. "How you doing so far?"

"I feel like a — "

"Careful now."

"I feel like I've been doing it all wrong."

"Then you need number two. Jesus was the perfect Servant, which we can't be. But he forgives us when we aren't, and that's called grace, right?"

Sophie nodded.

"So you can stop beating yourself up and keep on growing."

"I wish I was already grown."

"And miss all this fun? Are you kidding?" Dr. Peter grinned. "Wait 'til you hear number three. Have you ever played 'Mother, May I?'"

Sophie groaned.

"I take it you didn't like it that much?"

"It wasn't fair. Even if I said, 'Mother, may I?' every time, Lacie — she was always Mother — could tell me to take two giant steps backward or something."

"So there was nothing you could do except what you were told."

Sophie felt her eyes bulging. "Are you gonna say God's, like, playing 'Mother, May I?' with me?"

"No, thank goodness. But it can feel like it when Jesus says things like, 'For he who is least among you all, he is the greatest.' What's that about?"

"I don't know."

"That's where number three comes in. What does it mean to 'be great'?"

Sophie pulled a panel of her hair under her nose, and Dr. Peter waited.

"Being the best at something?" she said. "Being the first one to do it?"

"Like being at the head of the line when you're in first grade."

Sophie rolled her eyes. "Zeke thinks he's all that when he gets to lead the line."

"Does he get to lead it every day?"

The eyes rolled again. "Uh—no. We hear about it when he doesn't. He's all, 'It's not fair!'"

"Did somebody promise him fair?"

"Nobody ever promised *me* that!" Sophie said.

"Picture where you are in line right now in your Film Club."

"I'm totally at the back." Sophie closed her eyes and saw Vincent at the head of their imaginary line, with Fiona right behind him, and Darbie following with a camera.

"What's happening now?" Dr. Peter said.

"Mr. DiLoretto's taking Kitty to the head of the line because he thinks she's an amazing artist—I mean, she is."

"So he's bringing her from the back of the line—where she was when she was having chemotherapy."

The lump in Sophie's throat expanded to its all-time biggest.

"I know that look, Loodle. Don't go guilty on me."

Sophie opened her eyes. Dr. Peter's were saying, *I'm not kidding*. "It wasn't fair that Kitty got leukemia in the first place. It isn't fair that your sweet mama has to stay in bed until the baby's born. And it really wasn't fair that your friends shoved you to the back of the line the *way* they did."

"Then I have a right to be mad at them?"

"By the world's rules, you do." Dr. Peter lowered his head to look at her over the tops of his glasses. "But whose rules are we trying to play by?"

"God's," Sophie said.

"Bingo. And part of playing by his rules is that we have to go against what the world expects us to do sometimes."

"So I shouldn't be mad at Fiona?"

"You *are* mad at Fiona. She's taken unfair advantage of you, and she doesn't even seem to know it. God understands why you're angry, but he wants you to take this chance to practice the servant life."

Sophie dug her fingers into the pillow's cheek. "And just let her take all the credit and mess up the movie?"

"Why not?"

This time Sophie's eyes nearly bulged from her head. "Are you serious?"

Dr. Peter shrugged. "What else can you do? You can't take her place in line and knock her to the back. You already tried that."

Sophie's face felt hot. He hadn't been kidding—this *was* hard to hear.

"I know," he said. "Not fair. But in God's world, it's not about fair. It's about grace. He serves us by giving us forgiving grace, and we have to do the same for each other."

"Forgive her? That's it?" Sophie couldn't swallow the lump. "But won't she keep shoving me to the back of the line if I let her?"

"Ah!" Dr. Peter's eyes lit up like birthday candle flames. "That's just it. Who says you're really at the back of the line? You aren't the star this time, or the director, but didn't you help Fiona be a better star? Didn't you show Vincent something about directing without him even knowing it?"

Sophie squinted her eyes behind her glasses, so maybe she could see it clearer. "So, like, I helped them get ahead in the line?"

"You did. You're still using some of your best gifts, Loodle. The ones nobody sees. That might not put you ahead in the world's line — "

"But it pushes me up in God's line?"

Dr. Peter leaned forward, so his eyes looked right into hers. "Number four is the best part, Sophie. With God, there *is* no line. You're right where he wants you to be, even if you can't figure out why."

It was so much to think about, Sophie could hardly concentrate on her homework that night. When Lacie brought her the phone, she realized she'd been staring at a page of math problems for ten minutes without even writing any of them down.

"It's some guy," she whispered.

She gave Sophie a sly look as she left the room, which made Sophie want to roll her eyes right out onto the floor. It was worse when she heard Vincent's voice on the other end.

"We need to talk," he said.

Only Dr. Peter's words in her head kept Sophie from grunting at him.

"What about?" she said instead.

"I want you to start studying Fiona's part."

"I already know Fiona's part," Sophie said, trying not to grit her teeth too hard.

"Excellent," Vincent said, "because I think you might have to take over for her."

Sophie clenched the phone. "Why? Is she sick?"

"You haven't noticed how — uh — challenged she is?" Vincent's voice chipped off into some high place on the *challenged*. "The only scene she's ever done halfway good as Leona was the one today that you guys had already practiced."

Sophie chomped down on her lip. It would be so easy to slide straight to the head of the line right now.

"We have to film this weekend, starting Friday after school," Vincent went on, "and Fiona's not even close. Just be ready to do her part, okay?"

Sophie did grunt this time. Two answers shoved each other back and forth in her head. She couldn't say either one.

"Jesus?" she whispered later when she'd turned out her light. "I'm gonna try to do what Dr. Peter said, but this is way hard. I hope you have a double scoop of grace waiting for me."

Sophie woke up the next morning feeling like a rubber doll whose arms were being pulled in two different directions.

There is no line in God's world, she kept reminding herself.

But if that were the case, she wondered as she climbed off the bus in front of the school, how come it was so hard to *be* in God's world right now?

Johanna Van Raggs hurried up the steps in search of Leona Artalini. As much as she detested it, she had to fetch the imperious art expert's chamber pot and help her dress. Another day of grueling service. It was her God-given job, and she must do it well — even though she was certain she could have found her master herself by now, as smart as she was. Should she break her vow of silence and speak up — or stand by and let Leona Artalini make a bags of the whole thing? Yanking up her wool stockings and cinching tight the strings on her overdress, she hurried on. She wasn't sure, but perhaps it would come to her when she saw her.

But the chamber pot was empty, and Leona was not at her closet as usual. There was someone else in the room, grumbling into a wardrobe. "Excuse me, Madam," Johanna said, "but may I be of some assistance?"

"No!" said the young woman, and she slammed the wardrobe door and stomped away.

Sophie blinked and watched Darbie disappear around the corner, shoulders hunched up like she was beyond annoyed.

For a few seconds, Sophie thought she should go after her. After all, Corn Flakes talked about their problems to each other.

The lump swelled in Sophie's throat again, and this time she knew what it was.

It's a big ol' wad of guilt, she told herself. *Because I haven't talked about my problem to Fiona or any of the other Flakes.*

Jesus didn't tell them to do hard things without being there for them, Dr. Peter had said.

I hope you're right next to me, Sophie prayed, *because it doesn't get any harder than this.*

She was already composing the note in her head that she would write to Fiona when she got to class, but Fiona was absent first and second periods. She wasn't there when the girls were dressing out for PE either, and none of the other Flakes knew where she was. Sophie threw on her track pants and T-shirt and double-timed it to the gym to find Vincent. He was watching Jimmy shoot layups.

"I have to ask you something," Sophie said.

"Wait a sec. I'm calculating Jimmy's average."

Sophie grabbed him by his sweatshirt sleeve and dragged him off the court. Hands on hips, she said, "Did you already tell Fiona you were replacing her with me?"

"I haven't even seen Fiona," Vincent said. "But I'm gonna tell her when I do. I mean, that is, if you can do her part. We could do one big rehearsal in class today and then just shoot Friday afternoon and all weekend." His voice cracked up into the stratosphere. "You can do it—you're, like, the best actress in our whole group. I wish I'd picked you for the part in the first place."

Suddenly the balls that bounced around them seemed to be bouncing inside Sophie's head. How long had she waited for Vincent to get a clue and figure this out? She'd imagined herself nodding somberly and assuring Vincent she only wanted what was best for the project.

Instead, she grabbed a hunk of hair and gnawed at the ends. Somehow this didn't feel at all like she'd imagined it.

Coach Virile gave his whistle a blast, and everybody scurried to their lines for roll check. Sophie saw Fiona skitter into her place, and she grabbed Vincent's shirt again.

"Don't say anything to Fiona yet, okay?" she said.

"I have to tell her. I'm the director." Sophie followed his gaze in Fiona's direction. She looked like she was practicing her Leona stance in line. "On second thought," Vincent said, "you tell her. She'll take it better coming from you."

"Thanks," Sophie said. She wanted to curl her lip at him, Corn Pop-style. But at least this gave her a little bit more time to decide what to do.

Coach Yates, the girls' coach, came down the row and counted everyone off. After she moved past, Sophie whispered to Fiona, "Where have you been?"

"I had to go back to the dentist," she whispered back. "But Boppa helped me with my Italian accent on the way and back, so it was cool."

Sophie was for once glad that Fiona was a three and she was a four, so they were in different groups for the passing drills. It was almost worth it to be in a group with Julia, Tod, B.J., and Eddie, just so she didn't have to talk to Fiona yet.

Eddie passed the ball to Sophie first, soft enough so she could actually catch it. She did the required three dribbles and handed it off to Tod. She expected him to make some you're-so-lame face, but he turned his focus at once on B.J. and thrust it at her. It landed squarely in the middle of her face and bounced back.

B.J. plastered both hands over her nose, but blood was already gushing out.

"Dude!" Eddie said. "You didn't have to throw it so hard."

"I can't help it if she can't catch," Tod said.

Julia casually tightened her ponytail. "He didn't even throw it that hard. B.J. cries if she breaks a nail."

To Sophie it sounded like B.J. had broken her whole face. She was crying so hard, blood was spattering through her fingers.

"I'll take you to Coach Yates," Sophie said to her.

But Coach Yates was already there, yelling, "Nothing to see here. Everybody get back to practice."

"You did that on purpose," Eddie said to Tod when B.J.'s wails had faded into the locker room.

"You can't prove it," Tod said as if making somebody bleed was all in a day's work.

"So if it was an accident," Eddie said, "how come you didn't say you were sorry?"

Tod smiled with only half his mouth and tossed the ball to Julia. "Because I'm not," he said.

Eddie shook his head at him, and without a word he turned on a squeaky heel and headed toward Coach Nanini.

Julia dug her gaze into the back of Eddie's head as he went. "He's so gonna go tell Coach you said that."

"He'll be sorry then, won't he?"

Julia flashed a smile at him, and Sophie wondered if she was using those whitening-strip things on her teeth. She also wondered if they'd forgotten she was there. Just in case they hadn't, she picked up the ball and pretended to practice her dribbling. She could still hear them talking. She decided it must be all that practice being mute.

"He's not the one I want sorry," Julia said.

"So — why can't it be a two-for-one deal?"

"Whatever," Julia said.

"Hey, where's the ball?" Tod said.

It was all Sophie could do not to pass it right at his nose.

When Coach tooted his whistle for the end of class, Sophie rushed

toward the locker room ahead of the other Flakes. She still wasn't ready to talk to Fiona, and that whole bloody-nose thing had distracted her from making a decision. But before she could even get out of the gym, Coach Virile called out, "Hey, Little Bit. I need to talk to you."

Okay, so maybe Fiona would already be gone when she got there.

She met Coach Virile on the bottom seat of the bleachers. His eyebrows were hooding his eyes, which didn't look happy.

"How's your friend Darbie?" he said.

Sophie felt a little pang of guilt. "Um — she seemed kinda funky this morning, but I haven't found out what's wrong."

He nodded his shiny bald head, as if he'd expected that very answer.

"Do you think she likes being on the Round Table?" he asked.

Ew. How was she supposed to answer that?

"I'll take that as a no," Coach said. "I'm not trying to put you on the spot, Little Bit. I just want her to have as good an experience as you did on the council."

Sophie didn't even try to swallow the guilt wad in her throat. She'd never thought about whether Darbie was having a good experience. It had been too hard to think about Round Table at all.

"I think she's struggling with a project we gave her," Coach Virile went on, "and I wonder if you could help her with it. I know your friends all look up to you — as well they should." He grinned down at her. "You're very wise for such a Little Bit."

Only Dr. Peter's warning kept her from saying, *No, I'm the most selfish person in life!*

The locker room felt empty when Sophie got there. The only voices she heard before she could get to her row belonged to the Corn Pops. She stopped and let the words filter out to her.

"Are you serious?" B.J. was saying. Her voice was shrill.

"Totally," Julia said. "Aren't I?"

"Absolutely," Anne-Stuart said, with Cassie chiming in.

Sophie didn't even have to know what they were supposed to be serious about to tell they were lying their heads off.

"Tod only threw the ball so hard because Eddie made him," Julia said. "Everybody thinks Eddie's all changed and he's all like Mr. Sunday School now, but that's so fake." Her voice dropped so that Sophie had to inch forward to hear the rest. "He has something on Tod, only Tod won't tell me what it is — but it's so bad that Tod will do just about anything Eddie tells him."

"Including hit you in the face," Anne-Stuart said. Even from where she was, Sophie could hear her sniff. "Are you okay, B.J.?"

"I am now," B.J. said. "Now that y'all are my friends again."

Your friends? Sophie wanted to scream. *Are you* kidding *me*?

"I love that," Julia said. "And you know what? You're the only one who can save Tod for me."

"Whatever it takes," B.J. said.

"Go to the gate during lunch. We'll tell Eddie to meet you there. Tod will take care of the rest."

"We'll tell Eddie you want to work on your project for arts class," Anne-Stuart said.

"Why would I want to meet him out there for that?" B.J. said.

"We'll *handle* it." Julia's voice went tight.

"I don't have to go *outside* the gate, though, right?" B.J. said. She sounded like an egg about to crack. "I got in trouble that time I went to the store to get you candy."

"No," Julia said. "You won't be the one going outside. Just leave it to Tod."

"Oh, I get it," B.J. said.

So did Sophie. She also got that she had about two minutes to change clothes and get to fourth period. As soon as the Corn Pops clattered out, she scrambled.

The same math problems she hadn't been able to focus on the night before still stared her in the face during Miss Imes' class. All she could think about was whether to warn B.J., who might not listen, or alert Darbie, who might not listen either, come to think of it. There was no way to write Darbie a note, not under Miss Imes' pointy see-all gaze. And before Sophie could get to her when the bell rang, Darbie bolted from the room.

"We're having our Film Club meeting in here today," Miss Imes said as Sophie wove among the desks to go after her. "Mr. Stires and I want to get caught up on how this movie is coming together for Mr. DiLoretto's class."

Even as she spoke, Vincent stopped in the doorway, turned to look at Sophie, and said, "Perfect."

"Why perfect?" Fiona said.

"Come on," Sophie said, hauling Fiona toward the door by the arm. "Let's go get our lunches. We'll be right back."

With any luck, Sophie thought, they'd be abducted by aliens before they could return to Vincent and his grand scheme for fixing the movie and probably ruining everything else.

"We have to rehearse the last two scenes," Fiona said as she trotted after Sophie toward their lockers. "We don't have time to sit around jacking our jaws — and besides — I want to show everybody what Boppa taught me."

Sophie stopped short at the end of the locker row, and Fiona plowed into her from behind. Darbie was leaning against her locker, swiping at the tears that had the nerve to slide down her face.

"You're crying?" Fiona said. "You hardly ever cry."

Sophie gulped down her guilt and hurried to Darbie's side. "It's about Round Table, isn't it?"

"Yes!" Darbie cried. "I'm making a bags of the whole thing. I'll never be as good at it as you were, Sophie. I'm rotten compared to you!"

"What's going on?" Maggie said. She marched up to them and studied Darbie's face. "Did some Corn Pop do something?"

"Yes!" Darbie said. "I don't know! It's B.J. — who can keep up with whether she's in or out from hour to hour?"

"Darbie —," Sophie said.

"She blew me off the other day, so I scheduled a meeting for right now — and she isn't showing up again."

"Darbie, I know —," Sophie said.

"And now I won't have my Action Plan for tomorrow, and Coach Nanini and Mrs. Clayton will think I'm an eejit, especially since Sophie was so perfect when she was on it."

"Darbie, I can help —," Sophie said.

"You think you're just the best at everything, Sophie, and sometimes it gets a little sickening!"

Somewhere in the circle of Flakes that had formed around Darbie, there was a frightened poodle-yelp and a nervous giggle. A familiar voice thudded, "I don't think we're supposed to say stuff like that to each other."

"I know I've been acting all jealous and silly," Sophie said. She planted her hands on the sides of Darbie's face. "But you have to listen to me. I know where B.J. is, and she's about to get into big trouble."

Darbie's face went so white that her freckles seemed to stick out from her face. "Where? Should I go there? I don't know what to do, Sophie!"

"If you'd hush for a minute, she'll probably tell you," Maggie said.

"She's at the gate," Sophie said. "She's setting Eddie up for Tod to push him off the school grounds so he'll get in trouble — "

"Why?" Fiona said.

"Because Julia told her to, and B.J. thinks she's back in the Corn Pops."

Willoughby shook her head, curls flying. "I know them — they're just tricking her — "

"Go, Darbie," Sophie said. "Get to her and help her. That's what Round Table does."

Darbie nodded, but she didn't move. "Come with me, Sophie. I don't know what to say to her."

"We'll tell Miss Imes you had an emergency," Fiona said to Sophie.

Sophie didn't realize until she and Darbie were almost to the gate that the lump in her throat was gone. But once they got closer, B.J. looked like she had a supersized one in hers. She was leaning against the fence that separated the school's back field from the parking lot at the Mini-Mart. Although B.J. was bundled up from toboggan hat to suede boots, Sophie could see her shivering, and she was pretty sure it wasn't from the cold. Sophie linked her arm through Darbie's, since neither of them had stopped to put on a coat, and headed toward her.

"You do the talking, Sophie," Darbie whispered. "I don't know what to say to her."

But there was no chance for anybody to say anything. As Darbie and Sophie approached from the school side of the fence, somebody wearing a down jacket the size of a comforter and a black ski mask emerged from the bushes on the other side and crept toward B.J. from behind.

Sophie broke into a run, still dragging Darbie with her. Darbie got herself loose and dived for one of B.J.'s arms while Sophie grabbed the other one.

"Get off me!" B.J. cried.

"We had to get you before he did!" Darbie shouted back at her, jerking her head.

B.J. glanced back just as the down jacket disappeared into the foliage. It rustled as whoever it was tried to get untangled for a getaway. Sophie, B.J., and Darbie made theirs in the other direction, and they didn't stop until they reached the empty baseball field. The two Corn Flakes pulled B.J. down onto the bleachers with them.

"That was Eddie Wornom!" B.J. said as she wrenched her arm away from Sophie.

"Eddie Wornom's way taller than that," Sophie said.

B.J. got her other arm untangled from Darbie's. "Who else would act like he was going to pull me through the gate and get me in trouble?"

"I don't know exactly who *that* was," Sophie said, "but I know what the plan was."

Talking as best she could with her teeth chattering, Sophie told B.J. what she'd heard Julia and Tod say in the gym. B.J.'s face seemed to freeze harder with every word. She could barely move her mouth when Sophie was finished, and she said, "How do I know you're not making that up just to make me feel horrible?"

"For the love of Mike, B.J.," Darbie said. "If we wanted you to feel horrible, we would have let that blackguard drag you off school grounds and get you suspended for the rest of your life."

B.J. gave Darbie a long look, as if she'd never really seen her before. "Oh," she said. "I guess that's right."

"Of course it's right."

"So Julia and them really didn't try to make it so I could finish the project with Eddie and not flunk and also help them get Eddie in trouble . . ."

Her voice faded out as Darbie shook her head. And then she started to cry, with a stiff face, without tears. It looked like every sob hurt.

"What am I supposed to do without friends?" she said.

Darbie looked at Sophie, eyes expectant.

Sophie opened her mouth, and then she closed it. She knew what to say to B.J. But Darbie probably did too. She was doing fine so far, and besides, she needed to do it. For lots of reasons.

"Darbie can help you with that," Sophie said. "I have to get to class, but Coach Nanini will give you guys passes since you're doing Round Table business."

She wrapped her arms around her freezing self and started for the building. She heard Darbie's footsteps behind her.

"Psst! Sophie!" she hissed. "You're leaving me? What am I sup-posed to say to her?"

Sophie stopped and grabbed Darbie's hands. They were like cold little claws.

"Just tell her what you know about real friends."

"You mean, like our Corn Flake Code?"

"Great idea."

"But you're the one who's good at this, Soph."

Sophie turned Darbie around to face B.J., who was huddled on the bleachers like an abandoned puppy. "You can do this," she whispered. "I know you can."

As Darbie started toward B.J., Sophie broke into a run. There still might be time to make it to fifth period before the bell rang. Just before she got to the double doors, they opened, and Mr. Benchley emerged importantly into the sunlight. Julia was on one side of him, and Tod was on the other. Sophie slipped behind the trash can, thankful that they were engrossed in conversation and hadn't spotted her.

"Now, you're sure she said she and Eddie Wornom were going to sneak out the back gate."

"Oh, she was all proud of it," Julia said.

Tod stepped out in front of them and walked backward. "We should hurry. Eddie said they were gonna go right about now."

Sophie couldn't see Mr. Benchley's face when they went past, but from the way his back straightened into a pole, she knew he believed them.

That's okay, she decided as she tore down the hall toward the stairs. They're not gonna find anybody at the gate when they get there. Except maybe Colton Messik in a ski mask.

But Colton was just flying into Mr. Stires' room when Sophie got to the end of the hall. Just as the door shut behind him, the bell rang.

Sophie was late again. For the third time.

Mr. Stires looked like he would rather swallow a test tube than give Sophie

12

detention, but a rule was a rule.

"We'll see you tomorrow after school," he said.

"Okay," Sophie said. It really didn't matter what day life as she knew it ended and Daddy grounded her and took away the camera.

Sophie gasped, right out loud. Film Club was supposed to film this weekend. They had it all planned for two cameras. And if she was under house arrest, she couldn't be in the film. At all.

Mr. Stires gave the assignment, and Sophie hid behind her science book to try to figure something out — and to get warmed up. She was shivering from the inside out. Two notes fell onto her desktop, and she opened them with stiff, raw hands.

You didn't talk to Fiona yet, Vincent had written. *What's the deal?*

What happened out there? Fiona's said. *The meeting was weird. Vincent is all freaked out about something.*

Sophie didn't answer. She stayed hidden, tucked into a ball at her desk. Then Darbie came in, gave her pass to Mr. Stires, and scribbled a note, which she dropped on Sophie's desk on her way to the pencil sharpener.

Thank you SOOOOO much. I think I helped B.J., but I couldn't have done it without you.

Sophie peeked over the top of her book. Darbie's eyes were sparkling like sun on snow, and it was the first time Sophie had seen her smile in days. Things started to melt in Sophie's chest.

And that was when she decided what to do.

Give me twenty-four hours with Fiona, she wrote to Vincent. *If she's amazing by rehearsal tomorrow, I think she should keep the part.*

She didn't write down what would happen if Fiona wasn't amazing. She *would* be amazing, just like Darbie obviously was. And nothing could feel better to Sophie herself than that.

"Why didn't you write me back?" Fiona said after class when they were on their way to Mr. DiLoretto's room.

"Because we should talk instead," Sophie said.

She got Mr. DiLoretto's permission to take Fiona out into the hall. "Whatever it takes to get her up to speed," he said.

Sitting on the floor beside her best friend, Sophie told her the truth about everything. Fiona's eyes displayed every emotion known to the human heart, Sophie was sure. They filled up with tears, sent out anger sparks, and rolled right up into her head in disgust. But in the end, they looked deep into Sophie's and said, "Will you help me? I really want to do this."

"Will I breathe?" Sophie said.

Mama was thrilled when Sophie called her after school, and she said of course Sophie could go to Fiona's and work until eight o'clock, as long as she got her homework done. Math was all she had, and Fiona coached her through it. After that, it was nothing but Leona Artalini 'til Daddy picked Sophie up.

"You look like somebody took a hundred-pound sack off your shoulders, Baby Girl," Daddy said.

"Yeah," Sophie said. "But there's still some left."

On the way home she told him about the detention. When they pulled into the driveway, she watched him run his hand down the back of his head. That only meant he was thinking. Beyond that, she couldn't tell, and she couldn't stand it.

"So am I grounded for the weekend? Are you going to take the camera away?"

"It's hard to punish you when you were trying to help somebody," Daddy said. "This is a tough call. Let me review it with your mother."

Sophie bit back further questions. At least he hadn't just said, "Yes. Your life is over."

"I will say this, though." He swallowed Sophie's shoulder with his big hand. "Whatever your consequences have to be, I'm sure proud of you. You made a big sacrifice."

He wasn't the only one who was proud, Sophie decided when she finished her talk with Jesus that night. His eyes looked very, very kind again.

The next morning, Sophie met Fiona an hour before school started so they could work some more. They each got a restroom pass in every class so they could take five minutes at a time to work out Leona's trouble spots. That used up all their passes for the rest of the school year, but they agreed it was worth it. Fiona was showing definite improvement. They slaved during lunch, except for the time it took to try on the costumes Maggie brought in.

Sophie put on her ragged petticoat, laced up her patched-over dress, and tied on the cap that fit right around her face. When she looked in the mirror in Mr. DiLoretto's room, an impish Johanna Van Raggs — ready to skip around and duck behind things — looked back. Not like Fiona and Kitty, who could barely move in the brocade outfits Senora LaQuita had made for them.

"What's with the hips?" Vincent said as Sophie helped Fiona move sideways between the desks.

"Those are farthingales," Maggie said. "They're like big pillows tied underneath. It was the style."

"Ouch! Willoughby, what are you doing to me?" Fiona said.

Willoughby leaned down from the desk she was standing on and showed Fiona what looked like a metal-net cap spray-painted gold.

"I'm putting your hair up in this," she said.

"*Torture* was the style?" Jimmy said.

"I love my costume, Maggie," Sophie said. "Thank you."

She swayed back and forth and watched the strips of skirt make fun patterns over the petticoat. Then she stopped.

Who was going to play Johanna Van Raggs when the Film Club started filming after school? She wasn't going to be there. She had detention.

Maybe they could start with the scenes she wasn't in. But she was in all except two. And if they didn't get more than that done this afternoon and tonight, it wouldn't be finished by Monday. Besides, Daddy might ground her —

"Don't you all look class!"

Sophie glanced up as Darbie made her way through the costumed Jimmy and Nathan and Kitty and Fiona, patting the farthingales and teasing the boys about their tights. When she got to Sophie, she pulled her to a corner.

"B.J. is doing *so* much better, thanks to you," she said.

"You're the one who's doing it," Sophie said. "Don't tell anybody I had anything to do with it. You should have the credit."

Darbie shook her head. "There's one thing I don't have any idea how to help her with, and I'm desperate. Who knew I would ever want to help this girl, eh?"

"What's up?" Sophie said.

Darbie lowered her voice to a murmur. "She doesn't have a project for this class. She hasn't been cooperating with Eddie, so he's just done his own thing with da Vinci. She's going to get an F, which is wretched enough, but heinous when you don't even have any friends to cheer you up."

"No doubt," Sophie said.

Darbie brought her face in closer. "You have an idea, don't you?"

"Maybe," Sophie said. "I'll let you know."

There really was only one way for Sophie to help B.J. *and* keep her own group from getting a lower grade just because she'd gotten herself in trouble at a crucial point.

Still, she talked to Jesus about it during the lab in fifth period. It was a good thing Fiona, her lab partner, knew what she was doing, because Sophie wrote every figure in the wrong place and turned over a caddy of test tubes before Fiona took over. At least she thought she saw approval in Jesus' eyes.

As soon as she got to sixth period, Sophie went to Mr. DiLoretto's desk. For maybe the first time ever, he smiled at her.

"Looks like your hard work is doing wonders for our Fiona," he said. "Why didn't your group make you the director? Somebody made some bad decisions — "

"I want to give my servant part to B.J.," Sophie said.

Mr. DiLoretto looked as if he'd just been quick-frozen. Only his eyes moved to squint at her.

"You want to what?"

"If you would give me credit for helping Fiona, B.J. could have my part. It didn't work out with her partner, and I don't want her to get an F."

He thawed out enough to fold his arms and cock an eyebrow. "It looked to me like the reason it 'didn't work out' was because she was too busy hanging out with another group."

"She's changed now, though," Sophie said. "And it would help Darbie too—that's a whole other thing."

"Well, aren't you just the little fixer?" Mr. DiLoretto said.

"No," Sophie said. "It's just what I'm supposed to do right now."

For a minute he looked at her, and then he stood up and perched on the edge of the desk. "I think I was wrong about you," he said. "I hope people like B.J. and Fiona appreciate what you do for them."

B.J. and Fiona might, Sophie thought as she took a big breath and headed for her group. But she wasn't sure about everybody else.

When she told them what Mr. DiLoretto had agreed to, the Film Club stared at her like a group in a snapshot. Vincent was the first one to break with his cracked voice.

"The whole thing's gonna be ruined now!"

"The servant doesn't even have any lines," Sophie said. "You told me yourself it wasn't that important of a part."

"Yes, it is, Sophie!" Kitty said. "Nobody else could play it as funny as you."

"Especially not B.J.," Willoughby muttered.

"I was playing it *too* funny," Sophie said. "Fiona's the star. The attention should be on her."

Jimmy was wiggling his foot. "Can B.J. learn the part by, like, this afternoon?"

"We *have* to start filming after school," Vincent said.

"I'll help her all I can." Everyone turned to Fiona as she spoke.

"I know the Johanna Van Raggs part inside out," Fiona said. "I kept thinking Vincent was going to make me switch with Sophie, and I wanted to be ready."

Willoughby leaned in and whispered, "How's B.J. gonna fit into Sophie's costume? I don't mean to be rude, but—hel-*lo-o*!"

Nathan turned red.

Maggie grunted. "I can do stuff with safety pins. It's not that big a deal."

"I just wish you'd talked to me about it first," Vincent said, voice splitting in two. "I'm the director."

"Oh, for Pete's sake, Vincent," Darbie said. "It isn't about you, now, is it?"

While Vincent fumbled for an answer, Darbie snuck her hand into Sophie's and squeezed. Fiona was less subtle. She gave Sophie a big ol' thumbs-up.

Detention that afternoon was worse than any of the medieval tortures Vincent had found on the Internet and wanted to put in the movie. It wasn't that cleaning the science lab was so bad. It was knowing that her best friends were all in the art room, filming without her. Sophie had felt so warm and good during sixth period, even watching B.J. stumble clumsily through her new part.

But now she hurt.

Jesus is with me, she told herself. *I forgot where I was in line and just did the jobs he gave me. I'm serving the way he would have if he went to middle school.*

But she still felt like somebody had cut a piece out of her. It was going to be hard to fill in that hole.

So hard that she didn't really want to see the group when Mr. Stires let her go early. Deciding she would just watch the film with everybody else in the class next week, Sophie went straight to the front of the school to wait for the late bus. Daddy was there instead, sitting in his truck.

Sophie ran toward him with her heart coming up her throat. Was it Mama? Was the baby coming?

But he was smiling and waving to her, and Sophie slowed down. He probably came to make sure she brought the camera home. Maybe she could get it from Fiona tonight. . . .

"So did you serve your time?" Daddy said as she stood on tip-toes to look into his window.

"Well, here anyway," Sophie said. "I can go back in and get the camera from Fiona if you want."

"How are you going to film this weekend without the camera?"

Sophie lowered her heels. "You're not taking it away?"

Daddy shook his head. "What more could you learn from that than you've already learned from everything you've been through?" He shrugged. "That's the only reason we ever punished you anyway, so you'd learn." He grinned a little. "I'm not sure it's working with your brother."

"You mean I'm not grounded either?"

"No. That's what I came to tell you. If they're still working, you can go back inside."

But Sophie just trudged to the other side of the truck and climbed in. "I think I just want to go home now," she said.

"How come?" Daddy said.

"Because I think I need to cry," she said.

And then she started right there beside Daddy, who drove her home without asking any more questions.

Sophie did watch all the filming that weekend, and Vincent let her work with the actors. He didn't have much of a choice, as far as Sophie could see. They kept asking her, especially B.J., who wasn't as hard to work with as everybody had thought she'd be. In the first place, she couldn't say a word as long as they were filming. And in the second place, she seemed to use something she'd learned from the Corn Pops: if you don't go with the group, you get thrown out.

But that isn't true for us Flakes, Sophie thought as she watched Fiona go through a scene with B.J. for the thousandth time. Willoughby patiently tucked all of B.J.'s blonde bob into a cap too small for her. Nobody teased Nathan because he turned into a radish every time B.J. even looked at him.

We could get selfish and compete as much as the Pops and Loops, though, Sophie told herself. And then she smiled. *If we didn't have grace.*

They showed their film to the class on Tuesday, and they got a standing ovation. Even Colton clapped, until Tod and Julia glared at him. Sophie could see it in every Corn Pop and Fruit Loop face: they weren't finished with B.J. yet. Or Sophie.

"Why weren't *you* in it, Soapy?" Julia said to her at the end of the period.

"Are you kidding?"

Sophie turned to look at B.J., who had appeared beside her.

"She was the best thing about it, Julia," B.J. said.

She darted off then, but not before Sophie saw her chin tremble and tears fill her eyes. It was the first time Sophie ever thought she knew how B.J. might feel.

Darbie had done good work with B.J., Sophie decided. She was going to have to tell her that.

She wriggled through the crowd at the door to try to catch up to her. But it was Coach Nanini and Mrs. Clayton she ran into in the hall.

"Got a minute, Little Bit?" Coach said.

Sophie looked wistfully at Darbie's disappearing back, but she nodded. They were having a celebration party at Fiona's. She could tell her then.

"We have a proposition for you, Sophie," Mrs. Clayton said.

"What's a proposition?" Sophie said.

Coach Virile grinned. "It's an offer you can't refuse. How would you like to serve on the Round Table as an adviser for new council members?"

Mrs. Clayton almost smiled, which didn't happen often. "We heard you were wonderful with Darbie," she said.

"She did all the work," Sophie said. "Honest. She wasn't even supposed to tell you!"

"She didn't," Coach Virile said. "But she was about the only one who didn't."

"We heard it from Mr. Stires and Mr. DiLoretto."

"And you'll never guess who else, Little Bit," Coach Virile said.

Sophie didn't even try. There were way too many surprises happening.

Coach Virile shook his head. "She sure could've knocked me over with a feather," he said. "It was B.J."

"So what's it going to be, Sophie?" Mrs. Clayton said. "Will you serve with us?"

Sophie could feel all the lumps and hurts and shivers draining from her. Everything but her smile.

"As long as you put it that way," Sophie said, "of course I will." Because she was really beginning to like this servant role.

Glossary

amiss (uh-MISS) when something seems to be incorrect, or doesn't make any sense

appalled (uh-PAWLD) being really shocked — almost disgusted — when something happens

baroque period (ba-ROHK PEER-ee-uhd) refers to a time in the 17th century when art, music, and clothes suddenly became very frilly and detailed — some people might say *too* detailed

disdainful (dis-DAYN-full) when you think you're better than someone else, and look at them with so much disgust that you show your feelings on your face

farthingales (FAR-then-gales) called "French farthingales," these were stiff, crescent-shaped pads that fashionable women in the 17th century tied around their waists so their skirts would look wider

gibbon apes (gib-en apes) small apes with very long arms, and cute, hairless faces. They are known for their very loud calls to each other, which sound like crazed laughter

heinous (HEY-nus) unbelievably mean and cruel

kibosh (KI-bosh) putting an end to something you don't like; to vote an idea down

Medieval (meh-DEE-vul) something or someone from the middle ages, which lasted from the 5th century to the 15th century. This wasn't a happy time to live in, because of the painful punishments and disease, but there were kings, knights, and cool castles.

pratfall (PRATT-fawl) when you fall or land on your rear end in a really humiliating way, causing others to laugh really hard

remission (re-MIH-shun) when a disease, like cancer, disappears with treatment. If the disease doesn't come back for many years, the person may be cured.

repugnant (re-PUG-nent) something so incredibly offensive that it can make you very angry

repulsive (re-PULL-sehv) gross, disgusting, and so icky you feel ill just thinking about it

subtle (SUH-tul) so small or quick that you have to look really hard to notice it

Sophie. Yo – Sophie LaCroix!" Sophie looked up at her best friend Fiona

and blinked behind her glasses.

Fiona pointed. "Are you putting both feet into one leg of your sweats for a reason?"

Sophie looked down at the bulging left side of her PE sweatpants. Fiona sat beside her on the locker room bench, one magic-gray eye gleaming. The other one was hidden by the golden-brown strand of hair that always fell over it.

"Are you thinking up a new character for a film?" Fiona said. "Yes! We haven't done a movie in so long that the whole Film Club's going into withdrawal."

Sophie shook her honey-brown hair out of her face. "I wish that's what I was thinking about." She got untangled and pulled on her PE sweatpants. "I can't keep my mind off my mom."

"What's wrong with your mom?" Willoughby, another member of their group, bounded in and stopped in front of Sophie, brown curls springing in all directions. "Um, Soph? How come you have your sweats on backward?"

Sophie groaned and wriggled out of them again.

"Her mom's been in labor since early this morning," Fiona told Willoughby. "Sophie's a little freaked."

Willoughby's hazel eyes, always big to begin with, widened to Frisbee size. "Your mom's having your baby sister today? Why are you even here? Why aren't you at the hospital?"

"It could take all day, and it's not like Sophie could help deliver the baby," Fiona said. "She can't even get her clothes on right. Soph, your shirt's on inside out."

Sophie looked down at the fuzzy backward letters GMMS—for Great Marsh Middle School—and groaned again. "I'm not even gonna be able to change her diapers. I'll probably put them on her head or something."

"You put diapers on somebody's head?" At the end of the bench, Kitty's china-blue eyes went almost as round as Willoughby's.

Kitty was the fourth member of their six-girl group. She was just back from changing clothes in a restroom stall. Although she was finally sprouting spiky hair after her chemotherapy for leukemia, she still had a tiny hole in her chest. It let the doctors put in medicine and take out blood without sticking her every time. She always changed her shirt out of sight of the girls a few lockers down—the mostly rude ones Sophie and her friends secretly referred to as the "Corn Pops." Those girls decided what was cool. A hole in the middle of somebody's chest *wasn't*.

"What about diapers on her head?" Kitty asked again.

"She hasn't put Pampers on her little cranium so far," Fiona said. "But then, the baby's not born yet."

"Any minute now," Willoughby told Kitty. And then she let out one of her shrieks that always reminded Sophie of a hyper poodle yelping.

Kitty giggled and threw her arms around Sophie, just as Sophie pulled her T-shirt off over her head. A few tangled moments passed before Sophie could get it off her face and breathe again. By then, Darbie and Maggie, the final two, were there. Maggie shook her head, splashing her Cuban-dark bob against her cheeks.

"You can't wear your shirt for a hat," she said, words thudding out in their usual matter-of-fact blocks.

Maggie was the most somber of the group, but that was just Maggie. Although the lip-curling Corn Pops called them "Flakes" — which was where their very-secret name "Corn Flakes" came from — Sophie and her friends let each other be the unique selves they figured God made them to be.

Only at the moment, Sophie wasn't feeling unique. Just weird.

Darbie hooked her straight reddish hair behind her ears. "You're all in flitters, Sophie," she said.

Darbie still used her Irish expressions, even though she had been in the U.S. for more than a year. Sophie loved that, but she barely noticed now.

"Her mom's having her baby sister right this very minute," Willoughby told Darbie, with a poodle-shriek. "Our newest little Corn Fl — "

"Shhhh!" Maggie said.

Willoughby slapped her hand over her own mouth, and Sophie glanced down the row of lockers to make sure the Corn Pops hadn't heard. It didn't look like it.

Nobody outside the group knew about the Corn Flake name. Being a Corn Flake was a special thing, with a code that was all about behaving the way God wanted them to. The Corn Flakes had agreed a long time ago that they couldn't risk Julia and her group finding out and twisting it all up.

Still, it was hard not to talk about it, especially when it came to Sophie's soon-to-be-born sister. They had plans for making her the newest Corn Flake.

"Sophie's so nervous about the baby," Kitty said to Maggie, "she's about to put a diaper on her head."

"Of course she is," Julia Cummings said as she walked by. She was the leader of the three Corn Pops, who all rolled their eyes in agreement.

But that was all they did. The Corn Pops had gotten into so much trouble for bullying the Corn Flakes in the first six months of seventh grade, they didn't dare try anything. Or, as Fiona put it, there would be "dire consequences." That was Fiona language for "big trouble."

And now that her Corn Flakes were all around her, helping her get her shoes on the right feet, Sophie didn't feel quite so much like the pieces of her world had been mixed up and put back together wrong. A new baby was big stuff, but Fiona, Willoughby, Kitty, Darbie, and Maggie could make even that easier.

As the Flakes hurried into the gym, a whistle blew and Sophie jumped.

"Does Coach Yates have to toot that thing so hard?" Willoughby said. "Doesn't she know Sophie's mom is having a baby?"

"I don't think so," Maggie said.

Coach Yates, their PE teacher with a graying ponytail so tight it stretched her eyes at the corners, gave the whistle another blast.

faiThGirLz!™

2 corinthians 4:18

Faithgirlz!™–Inner Beauty, Outward Faith

Sophie Series written by Nancy Rue

Sophie's World (Book 1)
Softcover 0-310-70756-0

Sophie's Secret (Book 2)
Softcover 0-310-70757-9

Sophie and the Scoundrels (Book 3)
Softcover 0-310-70758-7

Sophie's Irish Showdown (Book 4)
Softcover 0-310-70759-5

Sophie's First Dance? (Book 5)
Softcover 0-310-70760-9

Sophie's Stormy Summer (Book 6)
Softcover 0-310-70761-7

Sophie Breaks the Code (Book 7)
Softcover 0-310-71022-7

Sophie Tracks a Thief (Book 8)
Softcover 0-310-71023-5

Sophie Flakes Out (Book 9)
Softcover 0-310-71024-3

Sophie Loves Jimmy (Book 10)
Softcover 0-310-71025-1

Sophie's Encore (Book 12)
Softcover 0-310-71027-8

Visit Faithgirlz.com—it's the place for girls ages 8-12

Available now at your local bookstore!

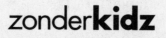

faiThGirLz!

2 corinthians 4:18

Faithgirlz!™–Inner Beauty, Outward Faith

The Faithgirlz!™ Bible

With TNIV text and Faithgirlz!™ sparkle! this Bible goes right to the heart of a girl's world and has a unique landscape format perfect for sharing! Ages 8 and up.

Hardcover
ISBN 0-310-71002-2

Faux Fur
ISBN 0-310-71004-9

Available now at your local bookstore!

zonder**kidz**.

We want to hear from you. Please send your comments about this book to us in care of zreview@zondervan.com. Thank you.

Grand Rapids, MI 49530
www.zonderkidz.com

ZONDERVAN.COM/
AUTHOR**TRACKER**